DISCOVERED INDISCRETIONS

DISCOVERED INDISCRETIONS

THE DISCOVERED TRUTH SERIES ROMANTIC SUSPENSE
BOOK THREE

JULIE BAWDEN-DAVIS

Roses
A R E
RED
PUBLISHING

ISBN-13: 978-1-7345012-0-9

ISBN-10: 1-7345012-0-0

Distributed by Roses Are Red Publishing

rosesareredpublishing.com

Created with Vellum

❀ Created with Vellum

ACKNOWLEDGMENTS

As they say, it takes a village. Here's my village. I'm supremely grateful to each of these fabulous people!

ARC Reading Gems

Julie Schlueter

Mandy Stanley

Pros

Sharon Whatley, editing

Judy Bullard, cover design

Kayla Curry, logo design

Kyle Kane, logo design

Sabrina Wildermuth, design consultation

Jeremy Davis, book design

To those who have loved and lost and found the courage to go on.

1

BORDER FIELD STATE PARK, IMPERIAL BEACH, CALIFORNIA

The water lapping the shore always calmed Brett Johnson—especially after he awoke from one of his nightmares. Lying on a damp beach towel on the wet sand, he drew in a big breath and let it sit for a second, slowly exhaling.

He'd gotten good at quickly steadying himself after a bad dream. It wasn't as easy to erase the familiar images from his mind. The look on his sister's face. But if he focused on the sound of the waves rolling in and receding, he could shut the door on the image.

Brett willed himself to think of the waves he'd soon be riding. A couple of hours before, he had dozed off after setting up a small camp to wait for first light and the best waves of the day. The ocean would wash away the memories. The seawater had a way of doing that as it seeped into his pores.

He raised himself up on his elbows and scanned the horizon, his eyes falling on the fence buried in the sand to his left, separating and guarding the San Diego and Tijuana, Mexico border. As the sun slid up out of the sea, casting its first light of the day, the wooden fence glowed.

Brett smiled, wiping his hair off his forehead and away from his eyes.

Soon the gulls would swoop across the horizon in search of their morning meals. Sometimes, if he listened carefully, he could hear their wings rustling as they lifted up to take flight.

Today, though, he suddenly heard something different. Shouts on the other side of the fence. A woman's voice. It sounded like she was pleading —begging even. Brett tensed and strained to hear.

"Ayúdame!" Spanish. That meant help. And he heard someone saying "no" repeatedly.

Just as he started to get up and check things out, something-correction-someone-tripped over Brett and sprawled across him. He stayed where he was as she floundered to regain her footing, letting out a string of Spanish cusswords as she did so. When she regained her equilibrium, she sprang to her feet. The woman wore a uniform and had her long black hair tied back in a ponytail. "Who the hell are you?" she demanded. "And why are you lying here like a piece of driftwood?"

"Me? Who are you?"

She whipped a badge out of her pants pocket and leaned over to stick it in his face. "ICE."

In response, Brett motioned to stand up, but she stuck a gun in his face.

"Stay where you are!" she hissed.

"I'm as American as they come," Brett said. "I don't think you need that gun for me, but you might need it for whatever is happening over there. He jerked his head to the shore where shouting had begun in earnest.

The woman lowered the gun and listened.

"I know that voice."

"Whose voice?" asked Brett.

"The woman's."

"The one screaming in Spanish?"

"Sí, gringo."

"Hey, don't shoot the messenger," he said. "I'm here minding my own business."

She checked out his towel and surfboard.

"I've got to see if it's her. You stay here," she ordered as she turned and headed for the fence separating the two beaches.

The shouting suddenly got louder.

"*Por favor, no!*"

Brett followed, stopping right behind her when she halted a few feet from the fence.

"Are you *loco*? I told you to stay," she whispered.

"Sorry. I don't listen well."

"Get down," she instructed, dropping to her knees and peering through a hole in the fence. Brett also crouched and found his own hole to look through.

About fifty yards away, he saw a woman being held by a giant of a Hispanic man.

"It *is* Ramona Valdez," whispered the agent. "*Ay, Dios mío.* And that man in the tux is Hector Hernandez." She looked at Brett, her eyes wide.

"If you say so," he said.

"That's the head of the Mexican mafia and his mistress." She muttered in Spanish. Something about talking to strangers and surfer bums.

"I usually don't talk to strangers, either," he replied. "But we appear to be thrown together."

She glared at him and put her fingers to her lips.

Both watched the scene unfold on the other side of the border. Dressed in a gold evening gown, the Latina woman the agent had called Ramona, struggled to free herself from a burly man who held her by the arms. Another imposing man restrained her companion, who wore a tux and looked as if he'd been beaten.

The woman and man holding her companion argued in Spanish, but Brett could pick up a lot of it.

"*Hector es importante.* They will kill you if you harm him!"

"They won't kill me, *mujer.* They will crown me," he replied in English. "There's a new *jefe* in town, and he wants to see you."

The man in the suit clutched his chest and stumbled, falling to his knees on the sand. His captor cried out, "Hector has a weak heart, Ramona. More reason to have a real man."

"Just leave him. Take me," Ramona cried.

Suddenly, the whine of a speed boat broke the early morning quiet, and the vessel quickly approached the shore.

"He has used up all of his lives," said the man, lowering the gun and shooting Hector in the forehead.

"Hector, no," wailed Ramona, wrenching herself free to run to him. She tried to throw herself on Hector, but the burly man grabbed her, unmoved as she thrashed and flailed in his arms. He dragged her to the waiting speedboat, her long black hair and dress becoming drenched in the surf.

The other man started to follow them to the boat but turned to survey the beach behind him. His eyes stopped at the point in the fence where Brett and his companion crouched, and he raised his gun.

"*Mierda*," said the ICE agent, pushing Brett's head down as a gunshot fired their way.

"*Vamanos*," the burly man called out from the boat.

"I saw something."

"We need to get out of here!"

Brett held his breath as the speedboat engine revved, and he soon heard the boat thudding over the ocean waves.

He and the ICE agent peeked up over the fence to see the speedboat heading away to the northwest toward Mexico. Neither spoke until the boat was a speck in the distance.

"What's your—" they both started.

"You first," said Brett.

"Who are you?"

"My name is Brett Johnson. And you are?"

She turned her back to the fence, let her knees sink into the sand and holstered her gun before replying. "My name is Tatiana Romero. And this is my beach."

"Last time I checked this was Mother Nature's beach, but okay. You mean this is your territory to patrol?"

She nodded.

"I've never seen you here before."

Tatiana eyed the surfer and took in the details. Shoulder-length brown hair, blue bathing trunks, and a surfboard. She hadn't noticed until now, but something about the way he looked made her feel intrigued, as if something clicked. For all she knew, though, he could be a smuggler. She was acting *loco*. And *loco* could get her killed.

"I need to take you in," she said.

"In?" Brett laughed. "On what grounds? I'm not about to miss these waves."

"I need to know why you're really here," she said, her hand moving to her gun.

"Look, I told you. I'm a surfer. I'm surfing this morning. Or at least I planned to. All of the good waves are being wasted." Brett looked out at the ocean as a wave came crashing to shore, its force spraying them. He licked his lips and tasted salt.

"You get into that water now, and you'll be sharing it with who knows what," she said, tilting her head back against the fence.

Brett glanced over her shoulder through the hole above her head and bolted up.

This caused Tatiana to rise and turn around to also peer through the fence.

"The body is gone."

"It can't be," said Tatiana, searching the sand with her eyes. It must have washed into the ocean."

"I don't see how. The surf hasn't gotten up that far yet."

He was right. Dead bodies don't disappear that quickly. Someone else had to be here on the beach with them. And that was a problem. While she was sworn to guard the border, she was also sworn to protect civilians. That meant she had to get this guy off the beach and out of potential danger—pronto.

Tatiana pulled out her gun. "We have to go."

5

"You'll get no arguments from me." Brett grabbed his towel and surfboard.

As if on cue, the sound of a gunshot filled the air near them. "Stay close to me while we get out of here," she told him. "You might want to leave that thing behind."

Brett rammed the surfboard under his arm. "To the parking lot?"

"Yes, let's go." Tatiana headed up toward the lot and Pacific Coast Highway, hoping they weren't heading straight into a trap.

When they came upon a van and Brett motioned to get in, Tatiana yelled, "Let's take my bike!"

He yanked the van's side door open, slid in the surfboard, pulled the door shut and turned to follow her.

Once at her nearby Yamaha, Tatiana grabbed a helmet and pushed it on, jumping onto the bike and turning the key in the ignition. She felt Brett hop on back and heard him shout, "Go north on PCH."

As the motorcycle lurched toward the highway, Brett grabbed onto her waist. Hoping he was hanging on tight as she accelerated to the max, Tatiana felt him lean into her, his breath warm on the back of her neck.

Hijole. What was she doing? She had a stranger literally at her back and was uncertain who might be following them. Fortunately, a glance in the mirror didn't reveal anyone coming after them. Brett was okay, she could tell, but he was hiding something. She had a sixth sense about these things and was rarely wrong.

Just when she thought that they'd outrun their assailants, Tatiana saw a black car in the rearview mirror. *Mierda*. She'd been worried about this when she decided to take the bike. It made for a fast getaway, but they were moving targets. She sped up even faster as they rounded a bend in the road, her mind racing to figure out her next move. When they came out of the curve, she spied a stand of eucalyptus trees on the right side of the road. Hold on tight, she thought, as she made a sudden sharp turn, plunging over the road's shoulder into a meadow and powering toward the trees. The cycle bumped over the uneven earth, sending them both up and off the bike's seat several times as they made their way to the trees' coverage.

Once inside the stand of trees, Tatiana slowed the cycle and shut it off. Putting the kickstand down with her foot, she got off and faced Brett, who remained seated on the back of the bike.

"We were being followed."

"I gathered that," said Brett, who turned to look from where they'd just come. "You think we lost them?"

"I hope so. That curve in the road was long, and they lost sight of us for a while. It'd be hard to get the car through the meadow without possibly getting stuck, but they could always come in on foot. I'm going to check the road. I'd tell you to stay here, but I know you won't listen."

She headed in the direction of the road, her hand on her gun. When they got to the edge of the trees, she stopped and scanned the road. A cargo truck and a jeep sped past. Otherwise, the coast seemed clear.

She felt Brett halt a few feet behind her. "I've never stopped on the side of the road and gone into one of these mini-forests," he commented. "It's quiet down here."

Tatiana listened. Except for the occasional echo of cars sweeping by on the road above and the sound of leaves crackling under their feet, it was quiet. So quiet she could hear Brett's breathing. That made her feel oddly comforted, yet uncomfortable, all at the same time.

"Yeah, well, I don't usually hang out on the side of the road, either." Her words hung in the still air, sounding silly now that she'd uttered them. Tatiana was glad her back was to Brett as she felt her face color up.

He laughed. "Good to know. I take it we're waiting to see if they come back?"

"We'll wait a couple more minutes and then assume they're still heading north and get out of here. How far to your place?"

"About another five miles."

"Great. Hopefully we can get there before they figure things out and double back. Where is it?"

"It's the first marina we come to. Coastal Cove."

"You live at the marina?"

"Yeah, on a boat."

Tatiana had a lot of questions about that but decided to table them. Best to get back on the road. She headed for her bike.

As they roared down PCH a few minutes later, Brett marveled at how well Tatiana rode. He preferred the water and the surfboard, but he'd ridden a motorcycle for a couple of years while in college. As they neared what some called Dead Man's Curve, he noted how she de-accelerated slightly and then leaned into the curve just enough to maintain speed and control. He enjoyed the ride as they sped along, willing himself to not think about the fact that a stranger with a gun was after them.

A few minutes later, as they approached Coastal Cove Marina, Brett pointed to the entrance. Tatiana slowed the bike, soon passing through the main gate, at which point Brett breathed a sigh of relief. In the parking lot that overlooked the marina and docked boats, she stopped the bike, but kept the engine running as Brett slid off the back.

"This is where you get off," she said.

Brett came around to the front of the bike to face her, shouting over the rumble of the motorcycle's engine, "And you're going to do what?"

Tatiana shrugged and turned off her motorcycle.

"You want to come in? Regroup? Call your boss or something?" asked Brett. "I've got a marine radio for emergencies. I'd call this one."

Tatiana's eyes narrowed as she studied Brett's face in the bright morning light. He was handsome, for a white boy. But what was he doing living here? That seemed sketchy.

"Are you going to stand there and profile me, or accept my invitation? I'm not used to running from bullets," said Brett, breaking the silence. "I'd like to sit down for a minute and figure out what the hell just happened."

"You live on water, *hombre*. Why is that? Don't you have a home?"

"This is my home. If you're done with your interrogation?" Brett paused, then turned and headed down the stairs toward the docks.

As Tatiana watched him descend the steps, she felt a pleasant rush of heat and then scolded herself. *Tati, cálmate.* She had better things to do, like figure out what to tell her boss about this morning's events at the border.

Tatiana decided to trail Brett to a blue houseboat named Carolina.

"Who's Carolina? A girlfriend?" she asked as they climbed onto the boat. "And how big is this thing?"

"No, definitely not an old girlfriend. Just someone I used to know. And she's a 40-footer." He unlocked the cabin door and stepped inside. Tatiana followed him in.

"You don't name a boat after someone you just used to know if the person wasn't important," Tatiana said as she assessed the small room, which seemed like a surfer's home. It contained a couch, table and chair, small galley kitchen, and a shelf with the marine radio. Pages from what looked like surf magazines were pinned up all over the walls—most featuring giant waves.

Brett pulled open a tiny refrigerator, revealing multiple water bottles and a few takeout containers. He pulled out two bottles and tossed one to her.

"I can get your call out with the marine radio, if you want. Have a seat." He gestured to the couch as he sat in the lone chair.

"I'm okay."

"Suit yourself." Brett opened his water bottle and chugged half of it down in seconds. Once finished, he said, "I'm no border patrol agent, but don't you have to check in with someone?"

"Yes, I do. Why so interested?"

"Oh gee, I don't know? Maybe because you're standing in the middle of my houseboat staring me down after we just witnessed an execution and then got chased by bullets?"

Brett watched as she pulled the band from her hair, letting it drop, dark and shiny sleek, over one shoulder. Afraid he was staring, he looked away and took a drink of water, trying to read his own emotions. She was a looker, there was no denying that. And he had a feeling what the uniform covered was even better. But they had bigger problems here. Like trying not to get killed.

"Technically we were chased by one bullet."

"And that's supposed to make me feel, what? Better?" asked Brett.

Tatiana threw up her arms and sat down on the edge of the couch.

"Not sure what to say?"

"I've only been with the border patrol for a year. I haven't had anything like this happen before. I want to call someone. But not my boss."

"Your boyfriend? Husband?" Brett was surprised to feel a flicker of disappointment.

Tatiana snorted. "I don't have either of those. And I wouldn't bother, anyway."

"Why not?"

"Because men are..." Tatiana trailed off.

"Hey, tread lightly there."

Tatiana laughed. "I want to talk to my old boss at the Huntington Beach PD."

Brett got up and headed to the marine radio. "Okay, give me the number."

"She's actually at the FBI now, but here it is." Tatiana recited the number and then took the receiver when Brett handed it to her. She smiled when Gisella's welcome voice came on the other end of the line after just one ring.

"Reyes."

"Gisella, it's me."

"*Tati! Qué pasa? Estás bien?*"

"I'm okay, but *tengo un problema.*"

"A problem, *mija? Qué pasó?*"

Tatiana described the execution at the beach and how she and Brett escaped, running from gunfire.

"I don't know what to tell my boss." Tatiana admitted. "Something told me to call you first."

"My advice? Be straight, *mija.* You don't want to run solo on this if there's people gunning for you. And remember, you're there to guard the US line. To keep people out. The murder was on Mexican soil."

"*Gracias*, Gisella."

"That being said, did you see who was murdered?"

"It was Hector Hernandez they shot. And they took Ramona Valdez."

Silence on the other end of the line.

"Give me your location," said Gisella. "And don't talk to anyone about this until I get there."

3

Tatiana set down the marine phone and glanced at Brett.

"What'd she say?"

"She'll be here within the hour."

Brett shot up from his chair. "The FBI? You kidding me?"

"It's just Gisella. Is that a problem?"

"Why would it be a problem. I thought I'd get some surfing and work in today, but instead I've got ICE up my ass, and now the FBI is coming here."

As Brett spoke, Tatiana noted how his head was a mere inch from the boat's low ceiling. She wondered how often he hit his head.

"Do you have anything to say about all of this?"

"How often do you hit your head on the boat's ceiling?" she asked. "It's pretty low for you. What are you? Six-two?"

Brett let out an exasperated sigh and flopped back down onto the chair.

Tatiana took a seat on the couch.

"Make yourself right at home." He made a sweeping gesture with his hand.

"You invited me in, remember?" She curled her legs under her and laid back against the cushions.

"I didn't know you were going to move in and invite your FBI friends."

"*Hijole*, okay, I'll call her back and tell her to meet me somewhere else, if this is putting such a crimp in your schedule." What did this guy have to worry about, Tatiana wondered? His tan?

"Forget it. She's on her way. I'll just go about my business while you wait." Brett made no move to get up.

"Your business is sitting there?"

"I'm thinking. Do you mind?"

"Thinking of something you could do to impress me?"

"Oh, yeah. I'm thinking, will scraping the hull impress her more than clearing the sewage?"

Tatiana fanned her face and scowled. "Wait on the sewage until I leave."

"Ay, ay, captain." Brett stood. "Can you get up for a second? I need to get out my computer."

Tatiana rose, taking several steps back to put some distance between them. As he kneeled on the couch and reached behind to pull the cabinet open, she admired his firm behind and felt a warm flush travel throughout her body.

After retrieving his computer and turning around to head to the table, he looked directly at her and asked, "What now?"

"What now what?"

"You have a weird look on your face. Anything else I should know?"

"Nothing, *hombre*. Just go about your day as if I wasn't here."

Brett soon discovered that going about his day as if Tatiana wasn't there was near impossible. He felt aware of her presence as he took his computer out of the case and plugged it into a socket under the small table. Once it powered up, he typed in his password and located the surfing article he needed to finish writing. Though he tried to think of the next sentence to write, a part of Brett's brain wondered what color polish Tatiana wore on her toes.

Tatiana watched Brett type and wondered what he was writing. She thought about asking him but suddenly felt the flattening fatigue that came every morning about this time. Her sign to climb into bed for a few hours. Soon, her eyelids got heavy and she dozed, periodically waking and peering out the boat window at the entrance to the dock.

When Tatiana finally saw Gisella walking down from the parking lot, she bolted up to go out and greet her. Hot and bright, the sun caused Tatiana to shield her eyes as she stood in front of the boat and watched her former boss approach. She hadn't realized how happy and relieved she'd be to see Gisella. Just the solid way she clipped down the stairs toward Tatiana made her feel better.

They had met on Tatiana's first day as a rookie at the police department. The two hit it off instantly. At the time, Gisella had been on the force for a decade and had made a name for herself as a street-smart cop.

Gisella wore a pair of dark slacks, a blue blouse, and a navy sports jacket. Tatiana knew that Gisella wasn't much for dressing up, so she probably used the jacket to hide the gun she carried. Ever since Tatiana had known Gisella, she wore her black hair shoulder length and often swept it behind her head in a big barrette.

Tatiana and Gisella hugged at the foot of the stairs.

"Tati, let me look at you," said Gisella, holding her by the shoulders and pushing her back slightly for better viewing. "You look a little tired, *mija*. But that's to be expected."

Tatiana hadn't realized until now how much she missed working with her mentor, her unwavering guidance center.

Gisella looked beyond Tatiana to Brett's boat. "Who's your friend?"

"He was there when everything went down on the beach."

Gisella raised her left eyebrow. Tatiana even missed that quirk of her mentor's. It translated to, *tell me everything*.

"I think he's okay," said Tatiana. "He's a surfer. He was waiting to surf in the early morning."

"You just met?"

"My gut says he's not involved in this at all. He seems pretty clueless."

"Hope your gut is right," Gisella said, stepping aside to let Tatiana lead them to the houseboat.

Brett got up when they entered the cabin. "Welcome to command central for trying to figure out what the hell is going on," he said. "May I offer you a beverage? I've got plenty of water."

Tatiana watched Gisella survey the interior of the small cabin and peer out the window at the bay on which the houseboat floated. "I see that." Then she gave Brett a brief once over and added, "We'll try to get out of your hair as quickly as possible. In the meantime, can you give us a minute?"

"Sure, I'll go get my mail. Check my horoscope to see what other surprises today is supposed to bring."

Brett left the boat and headed down the dock toward the nearby yacht club.

"A smartass," said Gisella, watching after him. "I like that." She took the chair and motioned for Tatiana to sit on the couch.

"First of all. How long do you have before your boss gets anxious about you not checking in?"

Tatiana checked the watch on her wrist. "About an hour."

"Okay, good. That'll give us some time to get your story straight."

Tatiana nodded, her curiosity now on overdrive.

"First, tell me what happened this morning. I need every little detail." Gisella took out a small notebook, but Tatiana knew from personal experience working under her that she probably wouldn't use it much. Gisella had a steel trap for a mind. Information went in and never left.

Tatiana described the morning's execution and abduction.

"What kind of a boat do you think it was?" Gisella asked.

"I might be able to identify it if I look at some photos."

"Good." Gisella shifted in the chair and leaned forward. "Tati, this is very important. Are you absolutely sure it was Ramona Valdez you saw taken away?"

"Positive. I saw her face and heard her voice when we were surveilling Hernandez during the Vargas case. I know she's been his mistress for several years now."

"Seven, to be precise," said Gisella, who began tapping the end of her pen on the notebook. "And you're sure you saw Hector Hernandez executed?"

"Positive. The man shot him point blank in the forehead."

"But then you said the body disappeared?"

"Yes."

"You didn't see anyone take the body?"

"No. The boat had just left, so we were staying down behind the fence on the US side until we were sure they were gone. It was actually Brett who saw that the body had disappeared. It wasn't long before the body went missing. Four—five minutes, tops."

"I need to talk to Brett, too. See if he has any other details to help piece this together," said Gisella. "What about the man who shot Hernandez and took Ramona? You get a good enough look at him to talk to a sketch artist?"

"Maybe. Brett may have, too."

"And then an unknown assailant shot at you?"

"Yes, I have no idea where the shot came from, so I think it would be hard to find a shell casing."

Gisella sat silently as she examined Tatiana, her eyes sweeping the younger woman's face. "You okay with this job, *mija*? I know it's a lot different to work alone. I've done it plenty of times, but you weren't used to it."

"I've been okay. I don't mind the alone time too much. The truth is, it's been pretty quiet on the shore until tonight. Before this happened, I had more of a chance of dying of boredom than anything else."

"How's your *abuelita*?"

"She's doing better. The rehabilitation at the home is helping a lot. My grandmother means everything to me, as you know."

Gisella nodded. "*Bueno*, so the pay raise to help with her recovery was worth the move to ICE?"

"Absolutely."

"Well, I'm afraid your days and nights of boredom are coming to an end for now."

"I had a feeling."

Gisella lowered her voice. "What I'm about to tell you is highly classified. You can't tell anyone about this. Understood?"

"Understood."

"It's critical we find Ramona."

"Okay," said Tatiana. "I'll do what I can to help with that. But what's the big deal about finding Hector's mistress?"

"She's not a mistress."

Tatiana waited.

"She's one of us, *mija*. An FBI deep undercover operative. She's been building a case against Hernandez for the past seven years. Being able to work the case more closely is the reason I decided to leave the PD for the FBI. Before this happened, we were literally days away from arresting Hernandez and his accomplices, including Vargas and the unknown person pulling their strings."

"*Ay, Dios mío*," replied Tatiana.

"You got that right."

4

"From what I've seen of Ramona, she's done an incredible job of playing the part of Hernandez's mistress."

Gisella nodded. "She is one of the best operatives I've ever seen. Since she's deep undercover, she checks in with her handler infrequently. The last he heard from her was about a week ago. At the time, things were okay. Obviously, that has changed."

"What do you want me to do?" asked Tatiana.

"Lay low and play it cool for now."

"You mean report to my boss that all was quiet last night?"

"Sorry, I know this puts you in a bind, but this can't get out. Ramona's life is at stake."

Tatiana sighed. "I understand. But what about the person shooting at us?"

"You let me take care of that. Call your boss right now, before he starts asking questions."

Tatiana got up and dialed the marine phone, waiting for Sergeant Maldonado to pick up.

"Boss, it's me Tatiana."

"Agent Romero. I was beginning to wonder what happened to you."

"Sorry, I had a little mechanical problem with my bike, but it's fixed now."

"I was thinking maybe there was some action on the beach last night."

Tatiana swallowed hard. Did he know something?

"You there, Romero?"

"Yes. No, nothing out of the ordinary last night, sir. Pretty quiet."

"Okay, good to know. Get some sleep. Kincaid is on duty tonight at the desk, if you need anything."

"Will do." Tatiana hung up the phone and turned to Gisella.

"We'll get this worked out as soon as possible, Tati. What time do you go on duty?"

"Nine tonight."

"Okay, I'm going with you."

If anyone else announced they would be going to work with Tatiana, she would have protested, but she knew better than to argue with Gisella. Besides, she was a little nervous about returning to her post alone after what happened last night.

Tatiana glanced out the boat's window and saw Brett approaching. He looked good, skin smooth and golden. Something about the solid way his body moved as he walked ignited a warm feeling in her belly.

"Why don't you go home and get some rest, Tati. I'll pick you up tonight for work."

"Meeting adjourned?" asked Brett as he entered and plopped down a pile of mail on the table.

Tatiana rose. "Yes, thanks for everything. I'm going to be on my way." She headed for the door.

"Wait. What about my van?"

"Your van?"

"Yeah, I need a ride back to my van."

"You don't have anyone else who can take you?"

Brett opened his mouth to reply, but Gisella interrupted. "I can take him. I need to look around on the beach and get his take about last night."

"Want me to go, too?"

"No, get some sleep. I'll see you tonight."

Fatigue pulling at her eyelids and making her feel as if she operated in slow motion, Tatiana left the boat without replying.

A few minutes later as she headed home on her motorcycle, Tatiana replayed the last twenty-four hours. Yesterday seemed so far away, and so much less complicated than today. She hated deceiving Maldonado. If it came out that she had lied, she could lose her job. And she really needed it. *Abuelita's* nursing facility was expensive. She felt a surge of the guilt following her around ever since she put her grandmother in the home. Then she reminded herself for the millionth time that there'd been no other solution. Once strong and indestructible, her grandmother had weakened in recent months. Doctors weren't sure what was wrong. They continued to check possibilities, though. All Tatiana knew was that she wanted to see her grandmother well again. She counted on her unwavering strength and support—and good advice. That advice had helped Tatiana innumerable times since she was a little girl.

Tatiana was leaving her fourth-grade classroom. Her grandmother waited outside, like she always did. When she saw Tatiana's bruised face, she cried, *"Qué pasó,* Tati?" Her grandmother took hold of her shoulders. *"Tu cara!"*

"Nada, abuelita. I want to go home."

"We're not going anywhere until I talk to your teacher about how you got hurt."

"Por favor, no abuelita!"

Her grandmother ignored Tatiana's pleas and marched her back into the classroom.

"You're probably wondering about Tatiana's bruised cheek, Mrs. Romero?" Tatiana's teacher, Mrs. Standish, stood erasing the chalkboard. "She didn't tell you what happened?"

"Please tell me," said her grandmother, who, unlike many of her peers, had learned English and taken the United States citizenship test.

"Tatiana got in a fight with another student, Roy. They were apparently arguing over who would use the slide next."

Abuelita peered down at Tatiana and frowned. "Is this true, Tatiana?"

"Yes, but he was making fun of you! He said he could ride the slide as much as he wanted, because you were a stupid wetback. So, I punched him." Tatiana looked up at her grandmother and thought she saw a slight smile teasing the corners of her lips.

Standing up straighter, her grandmother replied, "That is no reason to hit someone, Tatiana. You must say you are sorry to Roy."

"No, *abuelita*! I hate Roy. I'll never say I'm sorry. Ever!" Tatiana stomped her small feet and felt so much rage, she wished Roy was near, because she wanted to slug him again.

"Mrs. Romero, that won't be necessary. Tatiana and Roy will be working together during recess for the next several days on a project while being supervised by me. The activity is designed to encourage teamwork and cooperation."

That seemed to appease *abuelita*. "Thank you, Mrs. Standish. That sounds like a good solution. We will see you tomorrow."

Once out of the classroom, Tatiana stopped walking and exclaimed, "I'm just going to punch him again tomorrow!"

Abuelita swung around to face Tatiana, looking down at her with a serious glint in her eyes. "*Te quiero mucho, mi amor,* but listen to me. You will work with the boy, and you will shut your mouth."

"Bu—" Tatiana started, and *abuelita* gave her a warning glare. "You must be the one who doesn't react. The less you react, the more the other person will react, and the worse that person will look, *comprende*? You not saying anything will be the worst punishment for Roy. You will see."

Abuelita was right. The next day as they worked together and Tatiana refused to react, Roy became increasingly agitated to the point where he called her "a stupid wetback just like your old grandma." Mrs. Standish overheard and told Tatiana to go outside and play. Roy had to stay in during recess for the next two weeks. Afterwards, he steered clear of Tatiana.

What would *abuelita* say about what had happened this morning on the beach and how she had lied to her boss, Tatiana wondered? She pictured her grandmother's soft wrinkled skin and gray hair with streaks of her girlhood black still woven through. The eyes that Tatiana could never fool —that knew a lie before you could blink twice.

She slowed as she approached the driveway to her *abuelita's* two-bedroom house in Lincoln Park, which sat at the end of a cul-de-sac. She and her grandmother had lived in the sleepy neighborhood inhabited by mostly Hispanic families since her mother, who had a drug problem, left her at the age of six. Knowing what she knew now as a law enforcement officer about how important upbringing was in terms of a person's life, Tatiana felt even more grateful that her grandmother had taken her in all those years ago.

She stopped her bike in front of the garage door and shut it down. As she unlocked the padlock on the garage door and pulled it open, her thoughts turned to the conversation they always had about getting an automatic garage door installed.

"It would be so much easier for you if we had a garage door that opened automatically," Tatiana would insist.

"So much easier for me? Tati? You mean much easier for you," her grandmother would cackle and reply. "I don't drive anymore, remember?"

Unlocking the front door and entering the quiet house, Tatiana wished that her *abuelita* was home, so they could have the discussion again. Instead, she heard the grandfather clock ticking in the living room, a daily reminder of how *abuelita* was in a nursing home in nearby Chula Vista, where they annoyed the older woman trying to figure out what made her weak and dizzy. Tatiana was grateful that her new job afforded her more money, so she could pay for the expensive insurance deductible the home charged.

Tatiana threw her keys onto the small table in the home's entryway and yawned. She thought about taking a shower but was too tired to make the effort. Instead, she trudged upstairs to her bedroom, slid off her shoes and climbed out of her uniform. Lying down on her twin bed with the white and yellow woven-bedspread crocheted by her *abuelita,* she closed her eyes and immediately felt herself drifting to sleep.

Gisella and Brett drove in silence, making their way down PCH, which was stop and go as usual, he noted.

"You go surfing on Imperial Beach often?" Gisella broke the silence. Brett felt her steal a sidelong glance at him and knew she watched closely for his reaction. Probably making sure he was legit.

"Sometimes. I check to see where the waves are going to be best and then head wherever I can to get some good ones. Sometimes it's Imperial Beach and sometimes I head north to Solana Beach or Del Mar."

"Tell me your version about what happened last night."

"Most likely it's pretty much the same as Tatiana's. I got there about three in the morning and dozed off, waiting for first light to surf. The waves were supposed to be primo at about twenty to six. I had just woken up to the sun barely starting to rise when Tatiana tripped over me."

"Tripped over you?" Gisella turned to face Brett at that comment.

He grinned. This was obviously a bit of information that Tatiana had neglected to share.

"I was lying on the sand. It was still pretty dark. She probably wasn't expecting anyone to be there."

"And then...?"

"We heard a woman yelling. Tatiana told me to stay where I was and went running to the fence, so I followed her."

"You always listen so well?"

"Yep. Then we saw the argument and execution, and a boat make its way back out to sea."

"About how long was it before you noticed the body was missing?"

"Five minutes tops."

"And the gunshots were definitely meant for you?"

"Seemed like it."

A few minutes later, they pulled into the Imperial Beach parking lot. Gisella pointed to his van. "Yours?"

"That's her." Brett got out of her car and went to inspect his 1967 red VW bus. He sighed in relief to see that everything looked intact. No doors had been jimmied open or windows smashed.

"Mind showing me where you both were this morning?" asked Gisella, who had gotten out of her car and stood beside him.

They headed to the beach, which had filled with beachgoers on the American side and a few scattered people on the Mexican side.

Brett led her to the spot where he had been lying down, and he watched her examine the site. The indentation from his body was still there.

Brett then walked to the fence with Gisella following. When they got to the point where he and Tatiana had stopped, Gisella kneeled and peered through the same hole in the fence that Tatiana had used.

"Pretty good view from here," she said, turning around and looking up at Brett. "Was there enough morning light by the time you saw what was happening to see anyone's faces clearly? If I sit you down with a sketch artist, can you give enough details about the man who killed Hernandez?"

Brett dug in his jeans pocket and pulled out a piece of paper, unfolding it. "No need. I sketched the guy when I went to the clubhouse while you and Tatiana were talking." He handed it to her.

"You draw. That's impressive," she said, freezing when she looked at the face on the paper.

"You recognize the guy?" he asked.

"Possibly." She stood up, the drawing clenched in her hand. "I've got to get going. You good with your car?"

"Sure, thanks for the ride."

Brett gazed out at the ocean after Gisella left, wishing he was in the water. He probably missed some of the best waves of the month this morning. Too late now, he thought as he turned and made his way to his van. When he got back to the parking lot, he saw Gisella in her car having what looked like an animated conversation with someone on her cellphone.

He wondered where Tatiana was right now, and if she was still awake. What had gotten into him, he thought? Hopping into his van, he turned over the engine and drove out of the parking lot. As the van's wheels hit the pavement on PCH, he thought, now I can get back to my peaceful, quiet life.

5

Tatiana looked up at the ceiling above her bed. The ceiling with the hairline cracks she tried in vain to paint out of existence when she was sixteen. Within a few months of painting the ceiling with multiple layers of lime green paint, the cracks returned.

She glanced at the clock next to the bed, noting it was a little before five o'clock. Just enough time to take a shower and get dressed and rush over to her grandmother's nursing home to have dinner with her before meeting Gisella at nine. Tatiana swung her legs around to plant them on the wooden floor. First coffee.

As she measured coffee into a filter in the kitchen, she thought about Gisella and her new position with the FBI. It looked like Gisella was getting what she'd always wanted when they worked at the Huntington Beach PD together—better and quicker access to information. Her former boss would always get irritated when she couldn't get into a suspect's file because the FBI had sealed it.

Gisella liked to be able to work quickly and cut through red tape whenever possible. Tatiana understood that. Since joining ICE, she'd been amazed on several occasions at how quickly and easily she was able to access information on people she detained at the border.

She could get some insight into Brett, if she wanted to, she mused. But that would be an invasion of his privacy. And, besides, why look up someone she was most likely never going to see again? Tatiana poured herself a cup of coffee and slugged down half, plunking the cup down on the dingy Formica kitchen countertop. She had enough money saved to get the kitchen remodeled for *abuelita*, but the older woman refused to let Tatiana spend any of her money on the house.

Eyeing the clock on the avocado-green stove, she downed the rest of the coffee, then rushed to get ready. Fortunately, her grandmother's nursing home was only eight minutes away, so she would get there in time for the five-thirty dinner start.

When Tatiana arrived at the nursing facility nestled amongst giant oak trees, she parked and headed for the front entrance with its massive, reassuring front doors. She pushed her way in, comforted by the peaceful atmosphere in the home.

The receptionist greeted her as she passed and headed toward the dining room. The aroma of potatoes and onions made her stomach gurgle in anticipation. As she got closer, she heard the clink of utensils on plates and the murmur of conversations.

She spotted her grandmother in the expansive dining room that looked out over the gardens. This view had sold Tatiana when she went looking for nursing homes. *Abuelita* was a lifelong avid gardener.

Though her grandmother's back was turned to Tatiana as she gazed out at the view, the older woman must have sensed her presence.

"*Nietita,*" she said, calling her by the nickname she'd given her when her mother left Tatiana with her grandmother as a first-grader. It meant little granddaughter in Spanish. "I thought maybe your work had you busy."

"Never, *abuelita,*" said Tatiana, walking around to face her grandmother and leaning down to give her a kiss on both cheeks.

"*Bueno.*" Her grandmother smiled widely, her light brown eyes sparkling. "Sit down with an old lady and eat. I hope you brought your appetite."

"Of course." Tatiana pulled out her chair and sat down. She grabbed a piece of sliced French bread out of the bread basket, slathered it with butter and ate it in two bites.

"*Hijole, nietita*, when did you last eat?"

"I'm not sure," Tatiana replied with a full mouth, preparing herself for a lecture about taking care of herself.

"You know, if I was home, I could make sure you eat enough. And see that your uniforms are properly pressed, like I used to."

"Did the doctors figure out why you're having dizzy spells?"

"No, and you know that. You come to all of my doctor's appointments."

"Then what makes you think you can go home?" Tatiana took another piece of bread, spreading it thick with butter.

"An old woman could get stuck in here."

Tatiana sighed. "You're here for your own good. Soon they'll figure out why you are so dizzy and help you, and you can come home."

A waitperson arrived with a tray full of salads and gave them each a bowl. The greens were smothered in what looked like French dressing. Good. Her grandmother liked sweet dressing.

"Eat your salad. We wouldn't want you to wither away," she instructed.

Abuelita gave Tatiana her signature humph and dug into the salad. When they'd finished their first course, she said, "Tell me something exciting about your work. Catch anyone recently?"

The prior night flashed before Tatiana's eyes. "Sort of."

"Ahh, I understand, you can't talk about it. Did you go to the *quinceañera* and meet *Señora* Alvarez's grandson?"

Now it was Tatiana's turn to humph. "I told you I wasn't about to go to some stranger's *quinceañera* to meet a man."

"She's not a stranger. You know her from the neighborhood. It would have been good for you to show respect. A girl doesn't turn fifteen every day, *nietita*."

"Thank goodness," Tatiana muttered.

"I'm told her grandson is in the same line of work as you."

"I thought you said he worked for the government?"

29

"*Sí*, for the government."

"There's a lot of jobs in the government, *abuelita*."

"Never mind," her grandmother waved with her hand, dismissing the topic. "I'm just looking out for you."

"I know you care, but I think I can take care of my own dating life."

Abuelita laughed. "What dating life? You are referring to your work? Who do you meet while at work all by yourself?"

Brett flashed through Tatiana's mind, and her grandmother must have sensed something.

"You've met someone at your work, granddaughter?"

Tatiana wanted to change the subject but knew there was no point. Her grandmother always got the information out of her.

"Tell me," said her grandmother. "Give an old woman something to live for."

"There's nothing to tell," said Tatiana, relieved to see the waitperson coming with their main dishes. Maybe that would distract her grandmother.

"Look, *abuelita*, it's your favorite, chicken fried steak."

"My favorite is tamales, you know that. You're just trying to change the subject. But the chicken fried steak will do."

Tatiana took a bite as soon as the plate landed in front of her. She wanted to tell her grandmother about Brett, but she was superstitious about things like that. Afraid that if she opened up about her interest in him, it would all disappear.

For a time, they ate without speaking, until *abuelita* asked, "Will you tell me now about the new *hombre* in your life?"

Tatiana took a big drink of water and replied, "There is no new man. I met someone interesting last night who helped me with an incident at work. That's all. I doubt I'll ever see him again."

"Oh, you'll see him again." Her grandmother chuckled as she eyed the dessert tray coming their way. "Very soon."

6

It was two o'clock in the morning. Brett's sleep had been so erratic it led to his tossing and turning, which caused the boat to rock so much that he could hear the water slapping the hull and the boat creaking. Finally, exasperated, he got up and went into the kitchen. Pulling open the marine fridge barely large enough to hold a six-pack, he pulled out a beer that had sat in there for months. He wasn't much of a drinker, but right now he wanted something to help settle him. Removing the bottlecap, he took a drink and then went out onto the deck and sat down.

Despite willing himself to think of anything else, he'd been thinking about Tatiana and wondering how everything was going at the border. He even thought about going to the beach to catch a few waves at dawn but didn't want her to think he was following her. Besides, he was wary of surfing there, after what happened.

He sat down on the bench seat at the front of the boat, determined to clear his head. Swinging his legs up onto the opposite bench, he leaned back and looked up at the starry sky. Before he knew it, his thoughts drifted back to Tatiana, stomping around with her long ponytail swinging back and forth. He wondered, for the two-hundredth time, what she looked like under that uniform.

"Crap!" he said aloud to the quiet harbor. He took another swig of the beer and closed his eyes, forcing himself to focus on the sloshing sound of the water hitting the side of the boat as the vessel gently swayed. He'd be asleep in no time.

It was quiet at the border. Gisella and Tatiana had arrived several hours earlier in the post twilight. After they had looked around for any signs of people, they set up camp a few yards from the fence. Tatiana had unfolded a giant beach towel that she usually tripled up against the damp, snapping it out onto the sand so there would be enough room for them both.

She set down on the towel an ultra-powerful flashlight and a blowhorn for announcing her presence, should she get some border runners. Plopping down on the right end of the towel, she unscrewed the lid on her thermos and took a sip. She always brought herself black coffee sweetened with a little sugar.

"Black, no sugar," she said, handing a second thermos to her companion when she sat down beside her.

"Always good with the details, Tati," Gisella said, unscrewing the top of the thermos and taking a sip, then a big gulp.

For a time, they chatted about mutual acquaintances, then fell silent. That's what Tatiana had always loved about Gisella. The silence between them never created a void.

At one point, Gisella glanced at her cellphone. "Almost three," she commented.

"Like I said, it can get boring out here."

"Wasn't boring last night. Let's go over what happened again. You said Ramona and Hector were dressed up?"

"Yes. It looked like they'd been at a fancy dinner or something."

"Tux for him?"

"Yes."

"There was a tux jacket found about a mile north—caught in some rocks on the beach. I imagine it has to be his."

"What do you think happened to the body?"

"Most likely dumped at sea. The cartel doesn't like us to get the bodies. Autopsies could tie back to them. They prefer the hits as clean as possible."

"So, the shooter last night must have dumped the body."

"Most likely," said Gisella. "We identified him."

"How'd you do that?" asked Tatiana.

"Your friend drew a picture of him."

"Brett?"

"Yeah. Not a work of art, but it did the job."

"Who was the shooter?"

Gisella picked up her thermos and took a sip before replying. "I know this isn't your favorite subject. One of Vargas's men. He's new on the scene since our detainment."

"Our detainment? That's your nice way of saying when Vargas held us and beat the shit out of us?"

"Euphemisms are funny that way. Pisses me off less to say detainment," said Gisella.

"But you should be pissed! He could have killed us."

"Better to stay cool and calm. You know that. Only way to outsmart him. And believe me, I *will* outsmart him."

Tatiana knew she was right. Best to stay as objective as possible. They were silent for a time until Gisella broke the quiet.

"I hear your wheels turning. I can't tell you much more than I already did, but I can tell you this. We need to get Ramona back. It's vital on a number of levels."

"So, how is sitting here going to do that? You don't need to babysit me. You've got more important things to do. Go do them. I'll be fine. I had the best for a teacher."

That made Gisella smile. "*Gracias,* Tati. But I've got my reasons for being here tonight. We're expecting someone."

"I know this someone?"

33

Just as Gisella started to answer, Tatiana heard the whir of a motor-boat engine in the distance. Gisella stood up and pulled a small pair of binoculars from her pocket, peering through them out at the sea.

Tatiana rose. "Is it them?"

"I think so."

The boat got close enough to shore that Tatiana could make out its shape on the moon-lit water. The lights flashed four times.

"That's our signal." Gisella headed toward the shore, her hand on her gun. Tatiana followed and instinctively did the same.

As they approached, the moonlight bathing them momentarily became obliterated by a patch of dark clouds. When the moon reappeared, Tatiana made out two people on the boat. Seated, the driver looked dwarfed next to a hulk of a man, who shouted something, at which point the driver cut the engine. The hulk hopped out of the boat and grabbed the vessel with one arm, holding it steady as it buffeted back and forth in the surf.

Gisella had worn sandals, obviously in preparation for this. She took them off and cast them onshore, wading into the water, seeming to give no thought to the surf. Tatiana remained onshore with the surf nipping at the toes of her boots.

The hulk reached out his free hand to Gisella, who grabbed it, and they shook. Then she pulled an envelope out of her pocket, which he tossed to the driver.

Reaching over the side of the boat, the man pulled up a duffel bag from the deck of the boat and threw it over his shoulder. Then, as if working with a toy boat, he used his body to guide the boat around and point it toward the sea. Once he and Gisella headed toward Tatiana onshore, the engine turned on and revved as the boat scudded over the incoming waves, soon disappearing into the dark.

Tatiana smiled and watched as they approached. Their guest was about six-two with black, curly hair and creamy brown skin. He wore a dark red tank top that showed off his sculpted pecs that soon revealed the source of his nickname. She spied the familiar signature green, orange and blue macaw tattoo on his right bicep.

Once they stepped out of the water, Tatiana exclaimed, "Macaw, I thought that was you!" She reached out to shake his hand, but he pulled her to him for a quick hug.

"Always good to see you, Tatiana," Macaw's baritone voice carried over the waves crashing onshore. Tatiana had met Macaw a year before through Gisella, and at her request had helped him get across the border a few times when he lived in Mexico.

The trio headed toward the shore where she and Gisella had been sitting.

"How was your trip?" Gisella asked him.

"Bumpy, but quick. I caught a military flight out of Caracas. A buddy in the Air Force set me up. Then the trip from Tijuana to here tonight. Thanks for paying for the transport."

"You can thank the FBI. You're probably beat. We'll get you settled soon. I just want to make sure it stays quiet here tonight."

"This where they took Ramona?"

"Yeah, on the other side of the fence over there." Gisella pointed.

"As you know, Ramona and I go way back. She's good people. I can't stay too long, because I need to get back to Alexa. We're on a case right now. But I'll do what I can to get you pointed in the right direction."

"How is Alexa doing? And how's married life?" asked Tatiana.

"She's doing great. As determined as ever to save the world with her writing. I try to keep up."

"How's the work with ICE?" Macaw asked Tatiana, who always liked his deliberate, yet steady gaze.

"It's been fairly quiet until last night."

"So, Gisella tells me that Hernandez's body just disappeared. But you saw them take Ramona alive, right?"

"Yes, she was very much alive."

"That's good, but let's be honest. It's always convoluted and dirty and mean when it comes to the Mexican cartel."

Tatiana flinched, memories of the beating flashing through her mind. She hoped no one noticed. She eyed Gisella, who quickly piped in, "Of course, our main hope is that Ramona wasn't exposed and is still undercover."

"My guess is she still is," said Macaw. "With her looks, she's had the key players panting after her. To kill Hernandez and get his woman is a coup in their eyes. No one knows that she's just as smart as she is beautiful."

They talked for a little longer, and then Gisella left with Macaw with plans to pick Tatiana up at the end of her shift in the morning.

After they'd driven off, Tatiana relaxed a little, loosening her jacket slightly, so she could sit more comfortably on the sand. Just as she was taking a sip of coffee, Tatiana sensed someone behind her. She hadn't heard anything specific, but she could feel someone's presence. With short, tight movements, she slid her gun out of the holster, jumped to her feet and spun around, sending sand flying as she pointed her weapon and shouted, "Freeze! ICE!"

Before Tatiana stood a Hispanic boy of about twelve or thirteen, his eyes wide, his bare feet planted in the sand. He raised his arms at the sight of the gun pointed in his face.

Tatiana lowered her gun and looked around to see if anyone had accompanied him. She didn't see anyone.

"Where'd you come from?"

"I live around here, lady."

"I've never seen you before."

"I've seen you."

Tatiana's slid her gun back into its holster. "You can put your hands down. Where are your parents?"

The boy gestured behind him with the flip of his right hand. "They're home. Asleep."

"This is no place for a little boy."

The boy bristled. "I'm fifteen years old!"

Tatiana raised her eyebrows. "Even if that's the truth, which I highly doubt, you're still too young to be walking around on a dangerous beach at night. What's your name?"

"It's almost morning. I'm Chico."

"Okay, Chico. It's time for you to go home and get ready for school."

"I don't have school today; it's summertime."

Tatiana thought how the nearest houses were on Hollister Street, at least a mile away. "Where exactly do you live?"

The boy's eyes narrowed. "I saw you last night with your boyfriend."

"My boyfriend?"

"*Sí*, lady, that surfer dude."

"You were here? The whole night?"

Chico smiled. "Yeah, lady. I saw everything."

7

"First of all, what were you doing here? And I need to know exactly what you saw."

Chico looked down at his sandals and then at her as he spoke. "I think I would remember better if I had something to eat."

She glanced at her watch. "We'll get something to eat when my ride shows up."

"You don't have your motorcycle?" Chico looked disappointed.

"*Hijole,* boy. You here every morning?" Where were this kid's parents? Tatiana wondered as she heard a car pull up. Before long, Gisella approached from the parking lot.

"She your sister?" Chico asked.

"No, she's my ex-boss." Why was she telling the kid these things? She needed to keep her mouth shut.

Gisella walked up and looked from Chico to Tatiana.

"Babysitting?"

"I told you I'm fourteen," cried Chico.

"Fourteen? You better get your story straight. You said you were fifteen," said Tatiana.

"That's what I meant."

Gisella looked at the boy and raised her left eyebrow.

"Turns out he's willing to talk about what he saw here yesterday morning, if we feed him."

"Feed you, huh? Don't you eat at home?"

"I eat plenty at home. But you take me for pancakes, I'll tell you everything I seen."

"Sure, after you give me the names of your parents and their phone number," said Gisella.

"I don't remember their phone number."

Gisella sighed and rolled her eyes. "Fine. We'll feed you, and then Tatiana is going to take you home."

"The House of Pancakes is on Hollister Street. I like it there." They piled into Gisella's car with Chico in the back.

"Put on your seatbelt," ordered Tatiana.

When they were a block away from the pancake restaurant, Gisella got a phone call. After listening for a minute, she replied, "Got it." She put away her cellphone and announced, "Change of plans. I need to get to the office pronto. How about I drop you both off at that restaurant near your house, Tati?"

"What about my pancakes?"

"They have pancakes at the coffee shop," said Tatiana. "Better than the ones at the House of Pancakes."

A few minutes later, Tatiana and Chico got out in front of Aldo's Café. They went into the small diner to find a smattering of early birds nursing coffees. The air smelled of fried eggs and syrup. Chico shuffled his feet as they waited for the waitress to seat them.

Florencia, the morning waitress, called from the kitchen, "Go ahead and sit wherever you want. I'll get to you soon."

Tatiana walked to a booth by the window and slid into the seat facing the entrance. Chico sat down across from her, but she could tell that he had wanted her seat. He glanced back at the door.

"Expecting someone?" she asked.

"No, I just don't like my back to the door. *Mi papá* told me to always sit facing the way in."

"That's interesting that your father should say that."

"Yeah, well, he said a lot of things."

"Said?" Tatiana asked as Chico grabbed a menu out of a metal holder and opened it, ignoring her gaze.

She picked up another menu and pored over the options she knew so well. She'd get what she always did for breakfast. Huevos rancheros with extra cheese.

"You figure out what you want?" she asked, watching Chico examine the lunch portion of the menu.

"Where are the pancakes?"

"Not in the lunch menu."

Chico reddened. "I know! I was just seeing what they have for later."

"Later you're going to be home with your parents. Do you want eggs and bacon and toast with your pancakes?"

"Sure! All of it. And lots of syrup."

When Florencia got to their table, Tatiana ordered, then sat back in the booth. "Let's get to this, Chico. Tell me what happened last night. What did you see?"

"I seen you and your boyfriend falling all over each other. Then I heard a bunch of shouting, and you and the surfer guy, you both went to the fence. I couldn't see too good what was happening, but I heard a lot of yelling. I was up under the trees near the parking lot sitting in the dark real still."

Tatiana nodded for him to go on.

"When you and the surfer started running away, I heard the gunshot. I got really scared, and I laid down low, so he wouldn't see me."

"So, you didn't see his face?"

"No, I did see his face. He ran right by me when he was shooting at you."

"Would you be able to tell someone what he looked like, so they could draw the guy?"

Chico shrugged. "I think so."

Florencia arrived with their meals, setting an oversized plate in front of Chico. "A big meal for a big man."

His chest puffed up at her words. Then he dug into the eggs so quickly that Florencia added, "*Cálmate, niño*, you'll get a sore stomach." She turned to Tatiana. "Is he family?"

"No, he's part of something I'm working on."

"*Pobrecito*," Florencia clucked, walking away.

When Chico had eaten everything on his plate and stashed the Saltines in his pocket, Tatiana said, "We're going to your house before I take you to the station to see the sketch artist."

"No. My parents aren't home, and I don't have a key. They went to work by now."

"It's not even seven o'clock in the morning. And they always lock you out?"

"Can't I just go to the police station now, and then you can give me money for a bus home?"

"Is it unsafe for you to go home, Chico?"

"No. I told you. My parents are at work."

Tatiana sighed. If she brought him into the ICE office, that could put him in danger of being deported, if he wasn't legal. She tried Gisella's phone. It went straight to voicemail.

"I live right around the corner. We'll go there for now," she said.

The boy was quiet as they walked to her house. It gave Tatiana time to think about her next move. She needed to get a sketch of the shooter, but how? Then she smiled when she realized the perfect place to go.

When they arrived at her *abuelita's* house, Tatiana opened the garage and turned to Chico. "You get to ride on my motorcycle. Sound like fun?" she said with more confidence than she felt. If something happened to the kid on her watch, she could kiss her career goodbye.

Tatiana expected a smart comment from Chico, but instead he nodded vigorously.

She went to the garage wall covered in corkboard where her spare helmet hung. Taking it off the shelf, she handed it to the boy. "You ever been on a motorcycle before?"

"No, but I'm not scared."

"Good. Get on behind me and hold on to my waist, no matter what happens. And if you try to do anything stupid like stand up while we're riding, I'll shoot you for real." Tatiana closed the garage door and relatched it, then mounted her bike.

To her surprise, Chico had no retort to her statement. Instead, he dutifully got on behind her, locked his arms around her waist, and held on tightly as she turned on the bike.

Twenty minutes later, they arrived at their destination. Brett looked up from the deck as they approached. He held a cup of coffee in one hand and a newspaper in the other. Tatiana wished she had a camera to record the shocked look on his face. She stopped a few feet away, suddenly feeling shy.

It was Chico who broke the silence.

"Aren't you going to say hi to your girlfriend—surfer? I won't even look if you kiss her."

8

"This is Chico. Turns out he was there the other night when we were getting shot at."

Brett looked around the harbor to see if anyone else was outside on deck. "Let's talk about this inside the boat, okay?"

Tatiana shrugged. "Sure."

As she boarded the boat after Chico, Tatiana said, "I should have asked. Do you have plans right now?"

Brett turned the chair around and straddled it, crossing his arms over the back. "How can I help you?"

"Gisella said you did a sketch of the guy on the beach. Could you do a sketch if Chico tells you what the guy he saw running after us with the gun looks like?"

"Probably. If he gives me good details."

"Okay great." Tatiana stood up. "I'll be back in a couple of hours for him—three hours tops."

"Whoa!" Brett sprang up. "I have a few minutes for this, not a few hours for babysitting."

Chico sat up to protest—most likely about the babysitting comment—but Tatiana motioned to clamp her hand over his mouth, and he stopped.

"Please, Brett," she said. "I just need a few hours of shut-eye, and then I'll be back to take him to his parents."

"That's why you want to leave? To sleep?"

Tatiana nodded.

"Problem solved! You can sleep in my bed."

Tatiana paused. If that was the only way she was going to get sleep, she'd take it. "Okay, fine. Show me the way."

Brett pointed to the back of the boat, which was obscured by a curtain. "The bedroom and bathroom are back there. Me and Chico will go out on deck so you can get some sleep."

"Thanks."

Tatiana pulled back the curtain to reveal a tiny bathroom to the right with a toilet and shower and straight back, a twin bed in an alcove. Covered in a light blue bedspread featuring an anchor print, the bed had fluffy pillows and looked to Tatiana's tired eyes to be quite comfortable. She turned to pull the curtain shut and then ducked under the alcove and stripped out of her uniform. In her bra and panties, she slid in between Brett's surprisingly soft sheets. As she settled in, inhaling a hint of fabric softener combined with sea air, Tatiana visualized Brett lying in the same spot to sleep at night. That thought put a smile on her face as she drifted off to sleep.

Six hours later, Brett peeked in on Tatiana. Her dark hair lay fanned out on the pillow, and she had a slight smile on her lips. He realized he hadn't seen her smile much since they'd met. She had cracked a few jokes and laughed, but smiles didn't seem to come easily to her. She looked peaceful. He started to leave, when she shifted and opened her eyes.

"What time is it?"

"A little after four o'clock."

Brett entered and approached the bed, which made Tatiana's eyes fly wide open. He glanced at her clothing on the floor. "I wanted to talk about Chico out of reach of his big ears."

Tatiana sat up, her bare back resting on the boat's wall. Brett watched as she pulled the covers up below her chin.

"Did you get a good drawing?" she asked.

"If it's put through facial recognition software and the person is in the system, they'll probably be able to make an ID. The kid is as sharp as a fishing spear, and sneaky." Brett sighed and sat down on the edge of the bed. "To answer your question from yesterday—yes, the ceiling is a little short for me to stand."

Sitting this close to Tatiana in bed, Brett felt a current of excitement course through his body. The fact that she was mere inches from him dressed in nothing but panties and a bra distracted him for a moment, but he managed to ask, "Does the kid have a home?"

"I don't know. I just figured his parents were lousy, or he lived with a single mom. Crap. He can't be more than fourteen years old."

"Why don't we go tell him we're taking him to his parents and see what happens?"

"We?" Tatiana was surprised at how happy that pronoun made her.

"I just spent six hours with the kid. He's annoying, but he grows on you after a while, like mold on cheese."

Tatiana laughed.

"I like that."

"What?"

"Your smile. It's nice."

Tatiana tore her eyes away from Brett's. "I better get moving."

"While you're doing that, I'll check on Chico."

Brett ducked out of the room, pulling the curtain closed.

Just as she finished securing the last button on her shirt, Tatiana saw Brett's bare feet on the other side of the curtain.

"We've got a problem," he said.

"Give me a minute!" She jumped into her pants, then whipped the curtain back.

"He's gone."

"Chico?"

"He's nowhere in sight. I even got off the boat and looked around. And he took my spare cash."

"Shit! How much?"

"About four-hundred. Thank God he didn't nab my laptop, too."

"I can report it, but then missing persons and Social Services becomes involved," she said. "And we don't know for sure if he is homeless."

"Plus, they'll be asking you why you didn't take him home first, or call Social Services," Brett mused.

Tatiana sat down on the couch and pulled her cellphone out of her pocket. "Maybe Gisella will have some ideas as to what to do next."

She saw two texts. One from her boss, asking how last night went, and another from Gisella.

"I won't be asking Gisella anything," she said. "She and Macaw are chasing a lead. They've gone off the grid."

Tatiana stood up, then turned to face him. "Maybe Chico will show up tonight at the beach. I better let you get back to what's left of your day. And—"

"Yes?" They stood so close, Brett's breath hit her cheek. Tatiana's instincts were to find out what it was like to be hugged by him, but Tatiana was afraid where that might lead. Instead, she stepped back slightly.

"I mean it. Thank you. I know you had other things to do today."

"No problem," he replied.

That made Tatiana laugh. "You're a bad liar!"

Brett grinned. "I'm not lying when I say it was good to see you again. Oh, don't forget the sketch." Brett picked a drawing up off the table and handed it to Tatiana.

"I'll keep you posted," she said as she glanced at the drawing, then gasped.

"You know him?"

Tatiana felt the blood drain from her face.

9

Tatiana sat down on Brett's couch, struggling to compose herself. Seeing the photo set off a chain of memories that created a sharp pain in her side. Finally, she managed to say, "Gisella really needs to know about this."

"Considering your reaction, I'm more concerned about you. Who is this guy?"

Tatiana clasped her hands in her lap, her heart ping-ponging in her chest. "My last case at the PD was the roughest of my career. It's not the reason why I quit, but it helped me make the final decision." Tatiana stopped.

After a long moment of silence, Brett stood up. "Let me get you some water." He started for the refrigerator.

"Got anything stronger?"

"I had a beer in here, but I drank it the other night." He opened several cabinets. "I think one of my buddies left some tequila awhile back. That good?"

Tatiana nodded.

Brett took out two shot glasses and sat back down. Sticking the bottle between his legs, he unscrewed the lid, emitting the oaky hint of reposado into the air. Holding both glasses in one hand, he filled them and handed one to Tatiana.

"I was a bartender while in college," he said, as if an explanation. Tatiana drank the soft amber liquid all at once.

"You went to college?"

"Don't sound so surprised. Yes, I went to college."

"You get a degree?"

Brett took his shot and then held the bottle of tequila up. "Want another?"

"No, I have to work tonight."

He walked the tequila bottle and glasses to the kitchen. With his hands on the counter and his back to her, he answered. "No, I didn't finish. Let's put it this way. Life got in the way."

After a long silence, Tatiana finally asked, "That's all you're going to tell me?"

Brett turned around to face her. She saw a sadness in his eyes and immediately wished she hadn't spoken. "Let's get back to the subject here. Who is this creepy looking guy who shot at us?"

Brett was right. That man was dangerous, and he needed to know just how dangerous.

"His name is Carlos Vargas. When Gisella and I tangled with him, he was second in command for Hector Hernandez."

"The guy we watched get shot?"

"Yes. Vargas is known as the butcher. He cuts out your throat. We lost track of him after what happened."

Brett sat down again next to Tatiana. "So, what did happen?"

"There was some black tar heroin poisoning in Orange County beach communities. Lots of people were overdosing. After hauling in some of the likely suspects, we discovered the source—a dealer we took down. We thought we had stopped the stream from coming in. Then one night..." Tatiana stopped and took a deep breath before continuing. "One night, Gisella and I were headed out to get some dinner together when two men grabbed us right outside the station and forced us into a car. They drove us to an abandoned warehouse and tied us up and beat the crap out of us while Vargas watched. He made it clear we weren't to continue with the drug probe."

Brett gently put his hand on hers, which steadied Tatiana and helped her continue. "The good news was that we were a living message—they needed us alive to make a point."

He laced his fingers with hers. A simple gesture that soothed Tatiana, who hadn't told anyone about the experience until now. She sat in silence for a time, and then she spoke again, a sob catching in her throat. "Vargas stabbed me. So, like I said, he's dangerous. Which is why I need to let Gisella know."

Brett touched Tatiana's arm. "You need to take care of you right now. As far as I can see, Vargas is here, not wherever Gisella is. You don't know if he saw you."

"I have to go home and get ready for work. I appreciate you listening to me." Tatiana rose and moved toward the cabin's door.

Brett wanted to stop Tatiana—hold her and reassure her, but he was afraid to make the move. "Hold on," he said. "I'll get my stuff."

Tatiana turned toward him, eyebrows raised. "What for?"

"I'm going with you. And before you protest, I'm not taking no for an answer."

Tatiana opened her mouth to speak, but then shut it. Good, thought Brett. He didn't know what he would have done if she fought him on this. There was no way he was letting her leave alone right now after what she'd just revealed.

In his van five minutes later, he followed Tatiana to her house. He could analyze this—his need to keep her safe—or he could just go with the flow. Most likely, his therapist would want to do what he does best and analyze the situation. Ask if maybe he was overcompensating because of what happened with Carolina. He could hear his hmm when he told him about just meeting Tatiana and already helping her. But that was okay, because the truth was, he didn't care what his shrink said. For the first time in years, he felt alive. And as far as Brett figured, alive was a lot better than feeling nothing.

When he pulled up behind Tatiana at her house, Brett spotted the front door open. Before she could unlock her garage door, he rolled down the van window and called out, "Wait! Any reason your front door would be open?"

Tatiana moved around to the front door and pushed it open with her right leg, both hands tight on her gun. She stood in the doorway, scanning the room, which was in a disarray. Straining for any sounds, all she heard was Brett breathing behind her.

Entering the house, she checked all four corners of the room. The sofa had been upended and books pulled from the bookcase. Some of *abuelita's* prized ceramic knickknacks lay on the floor in pieces. Pointing the gun in the direction of the kitchen, she moved forward, careful to step over the debris on the floor. Cabinets gaped open and a drawer had been pulled out and upended onto the kitchen table. No one there, but the screen door to the backyard was open. They must have exited there. She moved to the small dining room off the kitchen and breathed a sigh of relief when she saw that *abuelita's* china cabinet hadn't been disturbed.

Gesturing to Brett with her gun, she pointed to the staircase off the living room that led to the second floor. As quietly as possible, she climbed the stairs with Brett behind her, stopping at the landing to listen. All she heard was the ticking of her *abuelita's* old grandfather clock. The short hallway had her grandmother's bedroom to the right, then the bathroom and then Tatiana's room. She eased open her *abuelita's* bedroom and entered. The contents of her drawers and closet were strewn here and there, but no sign of anyone.

Next in the bathroom, Tatiana spied the medicine chest open, pill bottles piled in the sink. The chest of drawers that held towels and supplies gaped open. They'd removed the lid to the back of the toilet. Most likely to see if she was hiding anything in the tank.

She left the bathroom and made her way to the last room in the house —her bedroom. Expecting to see the same level of disarray, she walked in and gasped. Her room looked like a typhoon had hit. Clothing and other personal items lay in piles throughout the room. Her mattress leaned against the wall, and her pillows had been sliced open, feathers coating the mess.

Tatiana spied her mirror and walked closer, her heart stalling as she read the words etched into the glass, "*Hola, Chica.*"

Vargas's calling card.

"*Gracias a Dios abuelita* wasn't here for this."

"*Gracias a Dios* you weren't here," said Brett.

10

"You going to call the cops?" Brett asked.

"I am the cops."

"I know that, but I'm thinking this is something that should be reported to the local PD."

Tatiana began picking up her clothing from the floor and setting it on the bed. Brett followed suit, reaching down to take a handful of clothing, which ended up including one of Tatiana's bras.

When she tried to grab it from him, he laughed.

"What?" she asked.

"This black lacy thing is as pretty as I imagined you'd wear," he said, looking at her.

"Maybe you're letting your imagination work overtime."

Brett threw his arms up, the bra swinging around as he did so. "Don't shoot! Yes, I'm guilty."

Maybe it was the sight of Brett standing there with her undergarment, or maybe it was her nerves on edge because of the house being broken into, but Tatiana started to giggle. Before long she was belly laughing so hard that she doubled over, gasping in pain.

Rather than look at her like she'd gone crazy, Brett laughed right along with her.

Finally, when neither could stand the cramping in their sides, they stopped laughing. Tatiana wiped tears from her eyes, and Brett commented, "God, that felt good."

"A little gallows humor does in times like these," said Tatiana. She glanced around the room.

"You think they're coming back?" Brett asked.

"I have no idea what they were looking for, or if they'll be back. I'm not even sure what this is all about."

"You can stay at my place until you figure it out."

She checked her watch. In an hour, she needed to be at the border. "I need to get ready to go to work."

"Okay, well, you got any eggs? I can cook us up an omelet before we go."

"We? You my bodyguard now?" Tatiana asked as she fished through a pile on the floor looking for clean clothing.

"Yeah, like that movie."

"As I recall, in that movie he had the gun, not her."

"We can trade."

"Forget it, *hombre*."

In the shower a few minutes later as the water rinsed off the day and prior night, Tatiana found herself thinking about Brett. She wished she knew more about him. A lot of cops she worked with at the PD would check people out the minute they met them. Although sometimes it was warranted, Tatiana didn't agree with the invasion of privacy. She'd be pissed if Brett did the same to her and found out about her mother. She shook herself out of her reverie and noticed that she hadn't rinsed the shampoo out of her hair.

Brett opened the refrigerator. Just as Tatiana had said, there were a dozen brown eggs. They looked like they were fresh. He also took out a half-gallon of milk, tortillas, and some sharp cheddar cheese. In a basket on the counter, he found a small white onion and discovered some chili peppers hanging upside down from a hook underneath the kitchen cabinet.

Pulling an old cast-iron skillet out from underneath the stove, he plunked it on a gas burner and turned it on. Then he found vegetable oil in a cabinet and drizzled some into the pan.

Brett rinsed the eggs and then broke four of them into a bowl with some diced onions and peppers and whisked everything with a fork. Adding a few dollops of milk, he mixed again. With a spatula he nabbed from a kitchen catcher near the stove, he folded the egg mixture as it cooked so that it'd be light and fluffy; then turned off the burner.

He was heating tortillas over the open flame of the stove when Tatiana entered the kitchen.

"Wow, I'm impressed," she said. "That's exactly how my *abuelita* heats the tortillas."

"Glad I can impress you with my culinary skills." Brett piled tortillas on top of each other on a plate. "How many you want?"

"As good as it smells, two," she said, coming up behind him to watch as he turned off the stove and got another plate out. Placing two tortillas on it, he filled them with eggs.

"Grater?"

"I'm not sure where it is."

"I take it you're not the chef?" Brett asked as he located the grater in the cupboard and quickly grated a nub of cheese onto her plate.

"Cooking is *abuelita's* department. Where'd you learn to cook?"

"My mother. She—" Brett stopped. "She was a good cook." He grabbed the plate and turned to face Tatiana, who stood her ground, rather than stepping back and allowing him to pass.

"Is there a reason you're literally in my face?"

"You were going to tell me about your mother and then you stopped.

Why?" Tatiana's closeness made Brett feel excited, but her question irked him.

"Your eggs are going to get cold."

"That's okay."

Brett moved in even closer, until they were eye-to-eye. "I've got a deal for you."

"I'm listening."

"You tell me about your mother, and I'll tell you about mine."

Tatiana narrowed her eyes. "We've got to get going soon."

"That's what I thought," said Brett, maneuvering around Tatiana and placing the plate of food on the table.

Tatiana got out some sour cream and plates and forks; then filled two glasses with water. She brought it all to the table. After they ate for a time, she spoke first. "These eggs are incredible."

Brett smiled, and Tatiana spied a chunk of egg on his cheek. Without thinking, she reached over to remove it. As her fingertips touched his cheek, she felt a rush of excitement.

"You had a piece of egg on your cheek," she mumbled, pulling her fingers away.

"Feel free to take egg off my face any day." Brett's smile turned mischievous.

Tatiana laughed and was about to reply, when her cellphone buzzed. She removed it from her waist and opened it. The number was Gisella's.

"Romero."

"Tati, it's me. I can't talk long. I need you to do something for me."

11

"My apartment. Desk, Tati...bottom. Paper with numbers...picture. Memorize...you must destroy."

"I can barely hear you," Tatiana spoke loudly. The reception was terrible.

"You want me to find papers in your desk and memorize and destroy them? What kind of papers?"

Silence and static on the other end of the line.

"Hello? Gisella?" She was gone. Tatiana hadn't even told her about Vargas.

"That was weird. I don't think I've ever heard Gisella not sound in control. Even when we thought Vargas was going to kill us. I think she wants me to go to her apartment and find some papers and memorize and destroy them. At least I think that's what she said."

"You got keys to her place?"

"Oh, shit! Was that what they wanted when they tore this place apart?" Tatiana ran up the stairs into her bedroom and jumped over a pile of clothing, kneeling next to her dresser. She reached underneath and breathed a sigh of relief when her hand landed on the duct tape. She could feel the key underneath. Ripping it off, she dropped it in her pocket.

"All good?" said Brett from the doorway of her room.

"Yeah, I got it," she said, standing up and patting her pocket. "We have just enough time to go to her place before I take my post at the beach."

When they arrived at Gisella's condo complex in San Clemente, just past the San Diego/Orange County line, Tatiana pointed to guest parking.

Brett parked the van and asked, "Want me to go in with you?" She started to tell him no, but then stopped herself. "Sure."

They made their way to Gisella's condo, number 337. Instinctively, Tatiana paused and listened intently at the door. No obvious sounds inside. She slipped the key into the lock and pushed open the door.

Once inside, Brett commented, "I bet this is what it's like in Gisella's head."

Tatiana laughed and looked around the living room area, which could only be described as austere and functional. The beige walls held no photos or works of art, except for a clock—its ticking sound echoing in the room. The closed dark brown window blinds matched the brown floor tiles, which were buffed to a shine. The room contained a black leather couch, two matching arm chairs and a coffee table that looked like it was made of cherrywood. The only item on the coffee table—a remote control—lay squarely in the center of the table.

"Her bedroom is back there," Tatiana said, heading past the kitchen—also gleaming and tidy. "If I recall, she has a desk in her room."

Sure enough, in Gisella's bedroom on the opposite wall of the bed sat a small black desk. Tatiana approached and began pulling open drawers. She had no idea what she was looking for and only hoped she'd know it when she saw it.

Brett came up behind her, and Tatiana sighed inwardly, welcoming the calm reassurance he radiated. She imagined leaning back and into his solid chest while he wrapped his arms around her.

"Anything?"

"No, nothing has jumped out at me."

"Did you look for a false bottom in the drawers?"

That's something Gisella would do! Tatiana pulled open the largest drawer, which brimmed with an uncharacteristic pile of junk mail and magazines.

"I'd say that's the drawer," said Brett.

"Yeah, me too." Tatiana leaned over and dug to the bottom, tapping until she heard a hollow sound. Then with her fingertips, she pushed until she felt the bottom of the drawer give slightly and slid the wood open to one side. Slipping her fingers into the space, she felt around until she found a piece of paper. Carefully, she pulled it out of the drawer.

"Good work," said Brett. "Let's see!"

Tatiana turned away. "Let me see what's in it first."

"I doubt it's a love letter or anything that would expose Gisella."

Brett was right. The document held a 9-digit number and a picture of a man. He was Hispanic, likely in his thirties, with close-cropped hair and laughing eyes. Something about those eyes seemed familiar. Finally, confident it was okay, she showed it to Brett.

"You recognize that guy?"

"I'm not sure. The string of numbers looks like a social security number. I need to commit it to memory, so give me a second."

After Tatiana was sure she'd memorized the numbers and the man's face, she went to the gas fireplace in the living room and burned the paper. "Let's hope I can remember that number when I need to," she murmured as she watched the flames lick the paper and then disintegrate it.

A few minutes later, they were speeding down PCH on their way to her post at the beach. Tatiana glanced at her watch. She would only be a few minutes late. She thought about the post, and how her favorite thing about guarding the border at the beach was listening to the soothing sound of the waves. She loved the sureness of the ocean. The waves always came in and went back out, no matter what craziness was happening onshore. A lot of the other agents hated the post, which is why as the greener ICE agent, she had it. They'd catch people coming onshore, who would then run back out and try to swim away. The ICE agent on duty often had to wade in after them, or if they went too far out, call in the Coast Guard. From what she'd heard, there had been a lot of drowning deaths at this post, due to the riptides. Fortunately, Tatiana hadn't experienced that yet.

When they got to the beach, they parked near the exit. If Chico was on the beach, she wanted to catch him unawares, so he wouldn't have a chance to run away. It was cloudy, so the beach was darker than usual. She and Brett made their way by the soft illumination of the parking lot lights.

"I think Chico hides out in those shrubs and trees over there." Tatiana said in a low voice as she pointed to a patch of vegetation on the edge of the parking lot facing the ocean.

They crept up, and she whipped out her flashlight, shining it into the interior of the shrubbery. No Chico, but there was an old sleeping bag and some tattered clothing.

"Looks like we've found his lair," whispered Brett.

"Yeah, hard to tell if he's been here since he left your boat."

They headed down to the beach near the fence where she usually held watch. Brett helped her spread out the big towel, and they sat down.

Tatiana yawned. "Crap. With everything going on, I forgot to bring my coffee."

Brett reached into his backpack and pulled out two thermoses, handing one to her.

"I might hire you after all." Tatiana took off the lid and sipped the coffee, mildly sweetened and with a hint of milk. "Perfect."

"So, I've got the bodyguard position?"

"I'll have to think on that."

They both sat without talking for a time, drinking the coffee and listening to the waves. Tatiana liked the companionable silence. It made her feel surer and steadier.

After a while, she spoke. "Looks like another quiet night. Good thing, since it's pretty cloudy and kind of hard to see."

"I would think there would be more people trying to cross the border when it's dark."

"They usually do."

"How many people have you stopped since you started?"

"At least four- or five-hundred."

Brett whistled. "That's a lot."

"It's not an easy job. I hate sending people back after all they've gone through to get here. I know they just want a better life. It's sad, really."

"Do some of them get mad at you because you're Mexican?"

"Like why would I send back one of my own?"

"Yeah."

"Sometimes. Many are mad about all the money they paid to the coyotes. It takes most people so long to save and borrow enough to make the trip. And now it's all been wasted for nothing."

Brett started to say something, but Tatiana spotted movement in the water. "I'm pretty sure that's a boat coming in," she said, springing up and grabbing her flashlight.

Brett followed close behind Tatiana as she moved slowly to shore, straining to hear. Nothing except for the water, but she could sense the presence of other people on a boat.

Stopping a few feet from the shoreline, Tatiana's breath became shallow and uneven. This was always the most nerve-wracking point, just before she exposed people in the bright light. She was never sure how many there would be. Or worse, if they'd have weapons.

Taking a deep breath, she swept the light across the water and yelled, "ICE!" With her other hand, she pointed the gun. "Don't move."

"Holy crap," said Brett.

Standing in the surf, eyes blinking from the flashlight's glare were Chico and a girl of about sixteen. They were waist deep in the water, Chico struggling to stay on his feet. So shocked was Tatiana to see Chico that she barely registered a boat's engine engaging as it pulled away.

"Don't shoot." Chico cried.

The girl looked at Chico and back at the light. Tatiana shined the flashlight behind them and to each side but didn't see anyone else.

"Come forward, both of you. *Ven!*" she yelled, when the girl didn't respond to English.

Tatiana and Brett walked backward as the two approached. When they arrived at the towel, Tatiana directed them to sit down.

"You have some explaining to do, Chico. If that's even your name."

"It's my name. Okay, my nickname."

"What's your last name?"

"Mendez."

"And what's her name?"

"Mendez."

"You're related to her?"

"She's *mi hermana.*"

"Your sister?" Brett finally spoke. "Is this why you stole my money?"

Tatiana shined the light directly in Chico's eyes. "Don't bother denying it Chico. Is this why? To get your sister across the border?"

"Yes! She had to leave. There's a really bad man in Tijuana who wants her to stay there. His name is el Diablo."

At the mention of the name, the girl let out a string of Spanish words, then started to cry, deep sobs wracking her body. Chico tried to comfort her.

"What'd she say?" asked Brett.

"That if she goes back, she's dead. But first they'll cut her throat out. I need to see the inside of her right arm, Chico." Tatiana instructed.

He whispered in his sister's ear. Slowly, the tears continuing to stream down her face, she turned her arm over and held it out. There it was blazoned on the underside of her forearm, a red, nasty burn in the shape of a V.

"Does that stand for what I think it does?" Brett asked.

"Vargas," said Tatiana.

At the mention of the man's name, the young woman wailed, "*No, por favor, no. Ayudame!*" She cried even harder.

Tatiana sighed. "Chico, tell her she's safe now."

"*Esta bien*, Rosalie, *estás seguro*," he told his sister.

She looked up at Tatiana, terror in her eyes. "*No entiendes! Vargas es horrible!*"

"She says you don't understand," said Chico.

"I heard her. I do understand," said Tatiana. "Believe me."

12

Tatiana walked toward the shore, trying to appear as if she was checking the water, but the truth was, she was freaking out. What the hell was she going to do? Protocol was that she should call this in.

Brett came and stood by her side. Tatiana dug the toe of her boot into the sand and kicked some up into the air.

"We could build a sandcastle."

"Humor isn't going to help," she said, but secretly appreciated his attempt. Tatiana glanced back at the brother and sister huddled together.

"ICE wouldn't consider the circumstances? She's obviously Vargas's property. That burn mark tattoo is proof."

"She could try claiming asylum, but there are so many girls like her coming from Mexico. The system is overloaded. If she was coming from a country officially at war, she'd have a lot better chance."

"Well…" Brett cleared his throat. "We can bring them back to my boat. Your house has obviously been compromised."

"Do you know what you're getting yourself into?"

"I feel bad for the kids. Look at them. They've obviously been through a lot."

She met Brett's gaze and felt her heart melt just a little at the look of compassion in his eyes. Could it be that he truly was a nice guy? Tatiana surprised herself at how much she hoped that was true.

"Okay, thanks, take them to your boat. And if you can pick me up at first light, that'd be great."

After convincing the young woman, whose name was Rosalie, she would be safe leaving with Brett and her brother, Tatiana tried to calm her emotions in order to think. There had to be a solution to this that would work out well for everyone. But the more she tried to figure it out, the worse the mess seemed. Just when her frustration level was about to boil over, she sensed movement on the beach.

"Shit," she muttered, standing up and pulling out her flashlight and gun.

Shining the light at the ocean, she saw what looked like a man swimming. When he gained footing and started to emerge from the water, she raised her gun and shouted, "ICE!" The man stopped in the surf and called out behind him as a warning, "*La Migra!*" Then he put his arms in the air.

Tucking the flashlight under her arm, she pointed the gun at the man with one hand while she reached into her pants pocket and extracted her cellphone. She hit speed dial on her phone to dispatch at the ICE office.

"You need backup, Romero?"

"Yes. I've detained someone trying to come in from the ocean, but there may be others further back in the water."

"Okay, dispatching the Coast Guard to the border now. The helicopter is in use several miles away, but there's a boat close."

Tatiana kept her gun trained on the man in the water, moving forward slowly.

"*Mi wife y daughter en la agua!*" He turned as if to go after them. "Wait, *espera!*" she told him. "*El US Coast Guard viene.*"

Just as Tatiana said this, a vessel approached, its lights flashing. "This is the US Coast Guard!" a man bellowed from a blowhorn. Powerful lights hit the water, illuminating two figures bobbing up and down in the surf.

When the man saw this, he turned and watched, standing firm, the waves buffeting his body. After several minutes, it looked like the Coast Guard rescue swimmer had the duo and was heading toward the boat.

"*Señor*, come to shore," she ordered. "They have your wife and daughter."

The man turned toward Tatiana and approached, his head down as he trudged through the water.

She kept her gun trained on him as she talked to the ICE dispatcher.

"I have the man. It looks like the Coast Guard has the two who were still in the water."

"Affirmative, Romero. We're sending an agent to take him into custody. Stay on your post."

"Okay, thanks. ETA?"

"Ten minutes."

"Over and out," said Tatiana.

"*Señor*, your daughter and wife are safe. They're being returned to Mexico. There are agents coming to return you to your family."

Keeping his eyes trained on the sand, the man continued to wade forward until he stopped several feet from Tatiana. No doubt he understood the ramifications of what had just happened. His wife and daughter were already on their way back to Mexico, but since he hit US soil, he'd have to go through the deportation process. If all of them had come ashore, she would have had them begging for her to look the other way as they escaped into Southern California.

A few minutes later, car lights lit up the parking lot. Tatiana heard a door open and slam shut and soon saw her colleague, Agent Meron, approaching. He'd been with ICE a few years longer than Tatiana and only worked the night shift once or twice a week.

"Busy night, Romero?" asked Meron as he came toward them. He was a husky guy with broad shoulders, a square jaw and a take charge way of walking onto a scene and sizing things up.

"You could say so. Apparently, this man's wife and daughter were in the water. The Coast Guard rescued them a while ago. He needs to be processed for deportation."

Meron stopped and put his hand on his holstered gun. "He said his wife and child were with him?"

"Yes." Tatiana had been about to lower her gun, but something told her to keep it trained on the man.

"Report is that there were two men picked up. They're known members of the Vargas gang. They're being held on prior charges. This one is likely a cartel member, too."

That caused Tatiana to grip her gun even harder as her heart sped up. "I thought you said you were with your wife and daughter?" she shouted, but the man continued to look at the sand.

"Keep your gun on him," said Meron. "I'm going to see if he's armed."

Tatiana nodded as Meron went over and patted the man down, pulling a knife from his pants that he put in his own pocket. Then he turned him around and cuffed him.

"You need backup?" asked Tatiana.

"No, I got him," said Meron. "Good catch. You earned some creds tonight."

As Meron yanked on the man's arm to lead him away, he finally looked up, malice in his eyes. But it was his words that made Tatiana gasp. "Vargas says *hola*!" He leered at her as he passed.

13

After Meron left with Vargas's man, Tatiana stood looking out at the ocean for a while, trying to stop the shaking that had started in her legs and climbed up her body. Hard as she tried, she couldn't push the images out of her mind of being held captive by Vargas and the beatings she and Gisella endured.

Tatiana took out her cellphone and dialed Gisella's number. Straight to voicemail. She sighed. Vargas had obviously sent those men tonight—to what? Kidnap her? Torture and kill her? She couldn't think about it, or she'd be paralyzed.

As she scanned the ocean for signs of more of Vargas's men, a flash of light swept across the sand. Tatiana turned around. A car pulling into the lot. Brett? She couldn't take any chances. Running to the border fence, she waited, gun drawn.

When she spied Brett making his way toward the beach, she exhaled, relieved. She fought the urge to run to him. Keep your shit together, she told herself. She was a trained agent, and she needed to continue acting like one. Instead she walked slowly toward him as he approached. They were a few feet away from each other when Brett's eyes flew open wide. She must have had a strange look on her face, because he asked, "What the hell happened? You okay?"

Tatiana was about to retort that of course she was okay, but to her horror, tears began streaming down her face. Brett took her in his arms and held her as she cried. God, how good it felt to be in his arms, which were so much more solid than she ever imagined.

When she was finally able to stop crying and tell him what happened, Brett used the edge of his T-shirt to wipe her eyes.

"Shit," he said. "This is serious."

"I tried calling Gisella, but it went straight to voicemail."

Brett looked out at the horizon, which had started to lighten. "It's almost time for you to be off. Let's just go."

Tatiana nodded, and she and Brett gathered her things and walked to the parking lot—Brett's arm hugging her to him.

Driving back to his boat, Brett glanced over at Tatiana and resisted the urge to tell her everything would be okay. For one, he didn't know that to be true. For another, he didn't want to get her angry. She had such a wall built around her. It seemed almost impenetrable most of the time—except for a few minutes ago when he'd seen her cry.

When they pulled into the parking lot at the marina, Tatiana said, "Thanks for everything. I'm sorry about back there. My breaking down— or whatever that was. I still don't understand why you're bothering to help me, but I'm not going to complain."

"Not many people help you in your life?"

"My grandmother and Gisella, but that's about it."

"What about your parents?" Brett said without thinking. He bit his lip, waiting for her to lash out, but she didn't.

Tatiana sighed. "My mother was a drug addict. She had me when she was eighteen. Thankfully, she lived with my *abuelita* when she was pregnant, who made sure my mother didn't do any drugs during that time. But as soon as I was born, she left for the streets."

"She still around?"

Tatiana shook her head. "She overdosed several years ago. That was really hard on my grandmother."

"And you, I would think." When she didn't answer, he went on. "What about your father?"

"I'm not sure who my father is. There were three guys my mother ran around with at that time."

"Do you know where any of them are?"

"I scouted them out a few years ago when I was at the PD. Two are ex-cons, and I couldn't find the third one."

"You connect with any of them?"

"No." Tatiana looked around, as if just noticing they'd parked. "We better go check on Chico and his sister."

When they got to the boat, they found Rosalie and Chico asleep on the bench in the kitchen. Brett indicated with his head toward the rear of the boat, and he and Tatiana tiptoed past and went through the curtain to Brett's bedroom.

"How about you rest for a while?" he whispered. "Get a little shut eye."

"That would be nice." Tatiana eyed the bed. "But what if the kids wake up?"

"I'll keep on top of them. They probably won't be up for a while."

"But you haven't slept yet, either, have you?"

"Don't worry about me."

"You've been really amazing." She gave him a warm smile.

They stood face-to-face in the tight space—so close that Brett felt a warm whisper of Tatiana's breath on his cheek. He could feel the quick hard beating of his heart.

"I meant what I said in the car," she looked up at him, her brown eyes earnest. "Thank you. I—"

Brett hadn't planned to kiss her. But when he leaned down to meet her soft lips, he recognized the hunger that had been building between them since the moment they met. He pulled away for a moment and asked,

"Should I go?" Tatiana responded by putting both hands on each side of his face and, without a word, pulled his mouth to hers. With the heat of her body pressed against his, he felt her desire, the passion that burned between them. Suddenly, everything seemed so right to Brett, so simple. His fingers slowly undid the buttons on her shirt, and it dropped to the floor. He unhooked her bra, and when her breasts were revealed, rosy-tipped and so beautifully soft and perfect, he felt a heat grow in his groin. She was trembling. He crushed his mouth against hers again, kissing her deeply, and then trailed his kisses along her neck to one soft, perfect breast. Greedily, he took one in his mouth, then the other. Tatiana's breath quavered. Brett picked her up and moved toward a blush of pale moonlight on the bed, when her phone buzzed.

"It might be Gisella," she said, reaching into her pants pocket for her phone.

"Unknown caller," she read out loud.

"Answer it." Brett put her down and sat on the bed in order to pull himself together.

Tatiana reached down to grab her shirt from the floor and held it against her. "Hello?"

"It's me, Gisella. What's been happening there?"

Tatiana explained what had transpired over the last twenty-four hours.

"I was afraid of this. I'm going to give you an address of a safe house in Oceanside. I want you to go there as soon as possible and stay there until I get in contact with you again. Take Chico and his sister with you."

Tatiana memorized the address, then hung up.

"Gisella wants me to take the kids to a safe house right away."

Brett nodded, looking away.

"About this," she said as she re-clasped her bra and buttoned her shirt. "This is obviously not the right time. Kind of a crazy moment."

The word crazy hung in the room. The last thing he needed was a relationship with a woman who stuck walls up left and right when things got close.

"Yeah, totally deranged," said Brett, standing abruptly and whipping the curtain back, which caused Chico and Rosalie to stir. "Let's get you all on the road, so I can go back to my non-crazy life."

"You're not staying with us?" She looked puzzled and gently took hold of his arm. He involuntarily tensed, and she removed her hand.

"Like you said, this is all crazy," he said. "I need to get back to normal."

14

Brett didn't say anything on the ride to the safe house, and the silence bothered Tatiana. On several occasions, she tried to make small talk, but he brushed her comments aside or just grunted.

"Look, I'm sorry. I'm not used to—" she finally said, then stopped.

What was it she wasn't used to?

Brett glanced over at her. When she didn't say anything, he refocused on the road.

"Aren't you going to say *anything*?" Tatiana felt like she was almost whining.

"You're the one in mid-sentence." Brett squinted into the rearview mirror. "Hey, I think someone may be following us."

Tatiana turned to look out the narrow window of the van. It was midmorning and the sun was bright. Still tired from the night before, Rosalie and Chico dozed.

"The black SUV?" Tatiana put her hand on the gun in her holster. Brett saw and commented, "If my van gets shot up, I swear, I'll—"

"You'll what?"

Brett just shook his head.

"Now who's the one mid-sentence?" Tatiana turned around to face the road. "Switch lanes."

"Could you manage a please in there?"

"*Dios mío!* Switch lanes, please." She couldn't believe she let herself get so distracted with Brett that she didn't notice they were being tailed.

Brett eased to the left into the center of the freeway. The SUV did the same.

"Damnit." She recalled the times she and Gisella had been tailed. She searched her mind for an option.

"We'll have to outmaneuver them. Wait until the exchange up ahead, where the 5 and the 78 converge. There's a stretch where there are no offramps. I think if we stop suddenly and swerve to the shoulder, the SUV will pass us. Then we can back up and head east on the 78 instead. From there I can get us to the safe house."

"That's a good idea," said Brett. "With all of the traffic at the interchange they probably won't see us doubling back."

"That's what I'm hoping. You okay with this?"

"Let's see. Am I okay with this? No, I'm not okay with any of this." He stared straight ahead.

Tatiana was about to shoot back a biting retort, but bit her tongue.

As they approached the interchange, a red Corvette tried to pry its way between the van and the SUV, but the SUV sped up and nosed it out. Soon enough, there were cars on either side of them and behind and in front of them.

Tatiana turned to Chico and Rosalie, who were awake now. "We're going to stop and go backward in a minute," she said in Spanish. "Hold on and don't worry."

Rosalie's eyes widened, but she nodded assent. Chico squared his shoulders.

At the interchange, Brett jerked the van to the right and they bumped over the gravely shoulder and came to a halt. The SUV sped by. Brett threw the car in reverse until they were back at the intersection of the 5 and the 78 freeways. Flipping on his hazards, he turned the vehicle around and waited for an opening, then headed east.

"For once, I'm glad for Southern California traffic," said Tatiana.

As they made their way through Del Mar Heights and then North City, Brett continued to check the rearview mirror. No one. Thank God. He glanced out of the corner of his eye at one point and noticed that Tatiana's eyelids had started to close. She kept her hand on her gun while she fought dozing off. Every few minutes when her head flopped forward, she'd shake it and sit up taller in her seat, sneaking a sidelong glance at Brett to see if he'd noticed. He pretended not to, although he couldn't hide the grin that threatened to pull up the sides of his mouth.

God, how she frustrated him! She was such a mass of contradictions. Prickly and defensive on the outside, but pliable on the inside when it came to certain subjects. She obviously had an allegiance to Gisella, and then there was the girl in the back seat. Here she was risking her life and her job to save her, and she knew nothing about her. Of course, her loyalty to her grandmother trumped almost everything.

Tatiana startled Brett when she put her hand on his forearm. "You okay?" he asked her.

"I just want to say thank you," Tatiana said quietly. "I know this wasn't what you signed on for, and I know it has totally disrupted your life, and even worse, this is really dangerous. But you're sticking with me—with it. Hopefully I can repay you some day."

"If we live through this, believe me, I've got a list for you."

"I'm sorry about taking you away from surfing, too. You really like it, don't you?"

"I love being out on the ocean, and waiting for a wave to swell and riding it in. Surfing keeps me sane."

"And now you're in the middle of insane."

Brett laughed. "Go ahead and get some sleep. I'll keep an eye out for anyone following us and wake you up if I see anything."

Tatiana took Brett's suggestion and let her eyes close. Before long, she was lying in bed in her childhood home, but she was maybe four or five. Sitting up, she crawled to the side of the bed and looked over the edge. Her mother was propped up against the wall, a needle in her hand. She was just about to put it into her arm when Tatiana cried out, "Mama!"

Tatiana woke suddenly, peering around the van to get her bearings. Brett looked concerned.

"Sorry. Bad dream. How we doing?"

"All's fine. We're about twenty minutes out. Do you need to talk about your dream? Or about your mother?"

"How did—?"

"You were talking."

"*Hijole*, I need to work on that." She was about to say more, when her phone started buzzing. Tatiana answered.

"Yes, who's this?"

"It's Macaw. Have you talked to Gisella recently?"

Tatiana shifted in her seat as anxiety took hold of her throat. "Not too long ago. Why?"

"I just talked with one of Gisella's coworkers in Cabo where I left her, and he said she was gone. No trace of her for the last couple hours. He sounded concerned. Said she left a message written on a coffee cup. Bolero. That mean something?"

Tatiana's throat went dry. She felt like a fish out of water struggling to speak.

"You there?"

"That was our code word for Vargas. He must have her."

15

Tatiana put her head in her hands. "This can't be happening again!"

"That doesn't sound good," said Brett.

"I'll tell you everything when we get to the safe house. How far?"

"We're in Oceanside now."

"They have food in the *casa segura*?" said Chico. "My sister needs food." Tatiana swung around. "You don't?"

Chico squirmed in his seat, but Rosalie's eyes remained closed. "They'll have something there," said Tatiana. "I assure you."

Tatiana turned back around and kept an eye out for the address she'd memorized. "That looks like it. A white house with a red roof."

Brett pulled into the driveway and shut off the van's engine.

"Chico, Rosalie, we're here. Wait for me to give the go-ahead to come in."

"You want me to go with you?" asked Brett.

"No, stay with them."

Tatiana went to the front door and found the lockbox Gisella had told her about behind a potted plant. Dialing in the code, she pried the box open to extract the front door key. She opened the door and stepped inside slowly, listening intently. No sounds of life. The place was musty—a combination of dust and disuse.

She drew her gun anyway and moved through the foyer and into the living room. A gray couch, an old television set, and an empty coffee table. She made her way into the kitchen and checked the back door. Locked. Nothing looked out of place. The faucet had a slow drip, but that was the only movement. Off the kitchen was a small dining room and then a hallway with two bedrooms.

Everything seemed to be clear. She peered through a window at the small backyard. She could see why they used this as a safe house. There was a tiny outdoor courtyard flanked by a 7-foot-high brick wall covered with climbing vines.

Opening the front door, Tatiana stood in the doorway and waved everyone in. Once all were inside, she shut the door and deadbolted it.

Chico went exploring immediately, leading Rosalie with him. From the back bedrooms he called out, "There's a bed for you and your boyfriend!"

Brett grinned. "Glad to see him back to his old self."

Tatiana laughed. "I have to admit I was starting to miss his smartass comments, but I'm sure I'll be taking that back soon."

"Who called?"

"Let's get them fed first."

Tatiana found some cans of spaghetti and corn in the cupboard. She and Brett prepared the meal together. She appreciated his staying next to her while they worked. He radiated a strength she needed right now. It took all she had not to let herself think about Gisella and what might be happening to her. She couldn't go there, or she would completely fall apart.

When the meal was hot, Tatiana pulled out some bowls and called out to Chico, who came in with Rosalie behind him. She looked a little calmer.

They all sat at the dining room table, and no one spoke as they ate. After devouring two bowls of spaghetti, Chico took a long drink of his orange juice, then slammed down the glass and asked, "What now?"

Brett turned to Tatiana. "We need to talk," he said. "You two go watch TV or something."

Chico started to speak but then appeared to think better of it. He gathered up his and his sister's bowls and headed for the kitchen, telling her in Spanish to come with him.

"Wait! Chico," Tatiana said. "Explain something to me."

The boy turned around.

"Why is your English so much better than your sister's?"

A look of fear raced across Chico's eyes, and he shifted his weight. Rosalie took the dishes from Chico's hands and headed to the kitchen, leaving him standing there.

"I need to know, Chico. This is important."

The boy looked down at the floor.

"Is she your sister?"

He raised his head and nodded hard. "*Sí*, I'm not lying about that."

"Go on."

Chico looked up, a forlorn look replacing his usual joking demeanor. He walked over and sat down where he'd been seated.

"Give it to me straight."

"I been here awhile." Chico stopped and picked at the tablecloth, while Tatiana and Brett waited.

"How long?"

"I think two years."

"How old are you?"

"Fourteen."

"How'd you end up here?"

"That bad man who had Rosalie. He got me, too, after our parents died in a fire, but this lady helped me get away and she brought me to a house with a family. Different young people lived there for a while before the lady found them someplace to go."

"What lady?"

The one on the beach.

"The other night? The lady with the man who got shot?"

Chico nodded. "She was helping me."

"Helping you how?"

"She came sometimes when I was living with the family and told me my sister would be coming soon, but it took so long."

"Where's the family?"

Chico began picking at the tablecloth in earnest.

Tatiana waited, sensing that if she pushed too hard, Chico would shut down.

He looked up at her, tears forming in his eyes. "*Muerto.*"

"Dead?"

"*Sí*, I went out to buy a soda. I snuck out the window in my bedroom. The people I stayed with didn't let me out at night. When I was coming back, I heard a man asking where the girls were. He said the lady and man in the house had to tell them, or he was going to kill them."

"The man and woman you were staying with?"

He nodded and wiped his wet cheeks with the backs of his hands.

"Are you sure they're dead?"

"I think so. I ran."

"Were there any children there?"

"No. They all left the day before. I was staying, because I was waiting for Rosalie."

"How'd you end up at the beach?"

"The last time she came, I heard the lady, Miss Ramona, saying that Rosalie would be coming on the boat, so I went to wait. But I needed to pay the boatman."

"And you needed money for that."

Chico snuck a quick look at Brett.

"How often did Ramona visit the house?"

"Only sometimes. Like every few months. She came from Mexico. Sometimes she brought more children."

"Okay, let me figure things out. Go watch TV with Rosalie."

"Holy shit," Brett said as soon as Chico was out of earshot. "You believe him?"

She shrugged. "Why would he lie?"

"What are you going to do?"

Tatiana threw up her hands. "I have no idea! This is only half of it. That phone call I got—I think Vargas has Gisella. I have to go get her."

"What about your job? Not to mention your life?"

"Don't you get it? Gisella is more than a mentor to me. She's like my mother!"

Brett pulled his chair close to hers and took her hands. "I get it. I do."

Tatiana looked into his eyes and saw that it was true.

"But there's no way I'm letting you go this alone," he added.

Relief and gratitude washed through Tatiana. "What should we do about Chico and Rosalie?"

"Does Gisella have a partner at the FBI?"

"Yes, his name is Gomez."

"Let's reach out to him for some help," said Brett.

"And what if he can't be trusted?"

"That's a chance we're going to have to take."

16

Tatiana waited for Gisella's partner to answer, hoping she wasn't making a mistake calling him.

"Yeah, Gomez."

"Detective Gomez? You and I haven't met, but I was Gisella's partner back at the Huntington Beach PD."

"Romero, right? She told me all about you. Funny you should call. I've been trying to track her down. You talked to her recently?"

"That's why I'm calling. I did hear from her earlier today. I—this would be a better conversation in person."

"Okay, come into the office."

Tatiana hesitated. It was apparent that Gomez didn't know she was at the safe house. But Brett was right. She had to trust someone.

"I'm at the safe house with the red roof."

Gomez's tone changed from conversational to concerned. "Gisella sent you there?"

"Yes."

"I have a meeting with an informant I can't get out of this afternoon, but once I'm done with that I'll be there. It'll be early evening. Hold tight."

"What'd he say?" Brett asked when she hung up.

"He'll be here this evening." Tatiana ran her fingers through her hair. "*Dios mío*. I should be on the road to find Gisella."

Brett reached out to rub her back. "You've got to figure out what you're doing first."

Tatiana's phone buzzed. She checked the screen, hoping to see Gisella's name.

It was her boss at ICE. "Shit, I was supposed to get my reports in by today."

"Hi boss. Sorry I didn't check in yet."

"Where the hell have you been? I expected you in this morning to close out the week."

"I had a family emergency."

"Your grandmother?"

"Just something I need to take care of. It won't happen again."

"Damn right it won't happen again. We both know a write-up on your record isn't going to look good."

"Agreed."

"Kudos for catching one of Vargas's men, but word is there's been other activity at your post."

Tatiana caught her breath. "Really? Not on my watch."

"I hope not, Romero. You have the makings of a good agent. I expect you in here after your next shift in three days."

"Yes, sir, I'll be there."

Tatiana ended the call and smacked her phone onto the table. "As if things couldn't get any worse."

She looked at Brett, whose eyelids were drooping. "Go get some sleep. Grab one of the bedrooms."

"You sure?"

"Have some nice dreams about surfing."

Tatiana tried to watch television with Chico and Rosalie, but the sitcoms only made her more restless. She dozed off a few times, but kept waking up, anxiety thrumming in her chest. She shouldn't be here babysitting. She should be on her way to find Gisella.

In the bathroom, she splashed water on her face—then gazed at herself in the mirror. Dark circles rimmed the underside of her eyes, and her frown lines seemed deeper. She rearranged her ponytail and patted the sides of her head with some water to keep the wisps at bay. Best to appear halfway put together for Gomez when he came.

As she walked by the bedroom where Brett slept, she heard a noise, so she opened the door a crack. Brett was moaning and thrashing around. She pushed the door open as quietly as possible and tiptoed in, stopping at the foot of the bed. Brett startled and sat up. "Carolina!"

That made Tatiana's heart dive. "No, it's me, Tatiana."

The glazed look on Brett's face turned to recognition, and he flopped down on the pillow.

"I didn't mean to wake you. I just wanted to make sure there wasn't anyone in here with you."

"It's okay," Brett said, wiping what looked like tears out of the corners of his eyes. "Bad dream."

"I'd say so," said Tatiana, fighting the urge to sit down on the bed. "Old girlfriend?"

He looked at her with confusion in his eyes. "What?"

"Carolina."

"No, she was my sis—. Never mind."

"Your sister?" That surprised Tatiana. She walked to his side of the bed and eased down next to him, examining his face as he clearly fought to wipe it of any vulnerability. She reached over and rubbed his arm. "You can trust me, if you want to talk."

"Can anyone trust anyone?" Brett blurted out, the look in his eyes a mix of anger and disbelief.

Tatiana withdrew her hand from his arm. Yet, she understood his words.

The look on Brett's face softened, and he sat up. "Look, I'm just tired. I know I can trust you," he said. "Someday I'll tell you about Carolina. For now, let's focus on what needs to be done. How long until Gomez gets here?"

Tatiana checked the watch on her arm. "Any minute."

"I'll be right out."

. . .

A few minutes later, there was a rap on the door. Tatiana peered through the peephole and was greeted by an FBI badge. She opened the door.

"That van outside yours?" asked Gomez. He wore a jacket and tie and had the same no-nonsense way of talking as Gisella.

"It's his," she said. "This is Brett. We were going to put it in the garage, but we got sidetracked. Why don't we sit in the dining room?"

Gomez eyed Rosalie and Chico as they passed the living room.

"So, you heard from Gisella?" Gomez said as they sat down. "She told me she had a good lead she was following and that she had backup, but I haven't heard from her in two days."

Tatiana took a deep breath and started from the beginning.

"Hell, that's bad," said Gomez when she finished.

"I know. I need to go get her."

"You need to stay here and do your job. I'll go get her—and Ramona. Any leads on where they're at?"

"Somewhere in the Cabo San Lucas area is what she told me."

"I'll send an agent here to take the kids to another safe house. Not sure if it'll be tonight or tomorrow morning. Then you're free to go back to your lives."

When Gomez left, Brett asked, "You trust him?"

"Not sure. What did you get from him?"

"He seemed genuinely concerned. I guess we'll know soon enough—when he brings back Gisella."

"I'm not waiting on that."

"What do you mean?"

"I'm going to Mexico to get her. I have the address where she's at. Macaw gave it to me."

17

Brett laughed. "You kill me."

"What does that mean?"

"You've always got a trick up your sleeve, or in your pocket."

Tatiana blushed. "Is that a compliment?"

"I think so." Brett paused. "You trust me to go with you?"

"Yes." Tatiana surprised herself at how quickly that came out. "But only if you want to. None of this is your mess."

"And miss the chance to help a badass former cop, now ICE agent take down a drug runner and trafficker?"

Tatiana's phone buzzed.

"Romero? It's Gomez. You okay to stay there with them tonight? An agent will get them first thing in the morning."

No, she wasn't okay with that, she thought. She needed to get on the road right away. But what could she do?

"Okay, thanks." She hung up and said to Brett, "Well, we can get some shuteye tonight. The agent isn't coming until the morning."

"You're not happy about that."

"No. God knows what's happening to Gisella while I'm stuck here babysitting."

"You don't know for sure that Vargas has her."

That's true, she thought. What did Gisella always say? Assumptions are like rotten eggs. Don't crack them open, and never eat them.

"I'm going to check on them," said Tatiana. She found the brother and sister curled up on the sofa with the TV on. She stepped over to turn it off, and then whispered, "You two go get in bed."

Tatiana watched them walk into the bedroom arm in arm and felt a knot in her throat. What was it like, she wondered, to have someone to lean on?

Just then, Brett came up behind her. "I'm glad that they're safe now."

"Me, too." Tatiana loved that he truly cared about the kids.

She wanted to turn and slide into his arms, but instead stood up taller, and turned around to face him. The way he looked at her, studied her almost, sent a shiver down her spine, despite the warm night. Something soft and unfamiliar seemed to take hold of her emotions.

When he reached out and touched her hand, it was like a signal. Unable to stop herself, she rose up on her tiptoes and wrapped her arms around his neck, kissing him full on the mouth, her tongue finding his. He drew back in surprise, then lifted her from the floor as she wrapped her legs around his hips. He held her there for a long while as she nestled her head in the curve of his neck.

"What am I going to do with you?" he whispered, continuing to hold her.

She looked at him, her mind reaching for a retort, but instead she found herself gazing into his sweet, blue eyes and marveling at how it felt to be held by this man. Secure and solid, enduring.

"Brett." She tried not to say what was in her head. She whispered the words. "Make love to me."

The words hung in the air. She heard his breath slow.

"Are you sure?" He let her slide down his body to the floor. His eyes earnest, hopeful, searching hers.

She took his hand and led him into the bedroom, shutting and locking the door behind them and sitting down at the foot of the bed. Brett knelt in front of her and started unbuttoning the buttons on her blouse, pushing it off her shoulders. Then he lowered her bra straps until her breasts were fully exposed. When he slid one hand slowly between her legs, she trembled at the intensity and fire he brought out in her. He guided her to lie back on the bed, and he unbuttoned her jeans. Lowering the zipper, he began kissing and licking her bare stomach and breasts. The heat of his mouth and strength of his strong hands on her body drove her wild with desire. A hunger for him, the strong, muscled, beauty of his body, jolted through her, and suddenly she wished everything to slow, wanting this moment between them to last all night.

She found herself laughing then, a high, sweet sound that echoed in the room. Full of joy and desire, she sat up and slid his shirt off, then kissed him passionately, her naked breasts pressed against his bare chest. She wanted to explore every inch of his body, and then start all over again.

"Let's take this to the shower," she suggested, after catching her breath. "We have all night."

"Great idea," he murmured as she got up and headed for the bathroom. Inside the small room, Tatiana turned on the shower, steam soon filling the room. Then she finished taking off her blouse and bra, sliding out of her pants. She stopped to stand there in her panties when Brett came in and began to disrobe. As he slid out of his pants, his underwear bulging, she felt a need for everything about this man to belong to her.

Brett picked Tatiana up and set her in the warm rain of water, stepping in next to her and pulling the curtain closed. He had wanted her from almost the moment he met her, and now, he wanted to savor every second, every inch of her.

Pushing her up against the wall, he raised her arms above her head and with his tongue teased each nipple of her breasts. When he let go of her arms and kissed his way down the center of her breasts and stomach, she stopped him, then placed the bar of soap in his hands. She turned, and he began to suds every inch of her, his hands lingering along the length of her back, her cheeks and down her long, beautiful legs. She faced him then and with rivulets of water streaming down her body, he gently washed her throat and shoulders, her breasts and stomach. Then he lowered himself to the shower floor, and as she tangled her fingers in his hair, he discovered her sweet spot, gently exploring, then going deep inside, over and over, until she cried out.

Brett stood up and raised Tatiana's right leg, the shower spray like tiny needles against his back as he entered her. He thrust slowly at first, then with an almost mad hunger, coming hard and fast deep inside her, crying out her name. They stood that way listening to the sound of the water and their own heartbeats. Then Brett smiled and leaned down to kiss her softly on the lips.

After they'd toweled dry, Tatiana found an oversized T-shirt in one of the bureau drawers and put it on. She unlocked the bedroom door and checked the rest of the apartment. All doors and windows locked. No movement outside. Cracking the kids' door open, she saw they slept soundly.

When she returned to the room, Brett looked at Tatiana through sleepy eyes and said, "All good?"

She nodded. "All's good, get some sleep." She smiled as she watched him drift off to sleep.

Sliding into bed next to Brett, she felt tired to the bone, but suddenly unable to sleep. The thought of Gisella with Vargas clenched her gut again. Though she always appreciated Gisella's guidance and support, she hadn't realized until now how much it truly meant to her. The thought brought Tatiana back to a morning many years before.

"Hija! Get me that cigarette there and *cerveza. Rapido!"* Her mother shouted at a six-year-old Tatiana. Morning light streamed through the frayed curtains in their one-bedroom apartment.

Tatiana knew what the beer smelled like, but this was a new kind of cigarette. She held it to her nose and inhaled. "Eeww."

"Give it to me." Her mother scolded her.

"Go make yourself some breakfast."

Tatiana went to the kitchen and climbed up on a stool. Standing on tiptoe, she opened the cupboard and pulled down a bowl and box of cereal. Then she went to the refrigerator. No milk again.

She poured herself some dry cereal, then screamed when a cockroach scurried out of the bowl and onto her leg.

"Qué pasa?"

"Cucaracha!"

"Callate and eat."

Tatiana shut up, but she didn't eat. Instead she sat at the table, bile in her mouth, and willed herself not to cry.

Tatiana chastised herself. There was no point to the memories. She knew that. They only took her to a dark place. She looked over at Brett sleeping peacefully and wondered. What was his life like growing up? Maybe there wasn't much to tell. He lived on a boat, and he obviously had some money. Maybe his parents were wealthy. She wouldn't be surprised.

Curiosity took ahold of her as she realized she didn't know his last name. She slipped out of bed and padded softly to his pants. Sliding his wallet out of the back pocket, she left the room, gently closing the door behind her.

She sat down at the kitchen table. When she opened his wallet, she saw the tip of a photo and slid it out carefully. She smiled when she saw a younger Brett and a girl who looked just like him. They appeared close in age. Same brown hair. Same bright blue eyes. Same lighthearted grin. They were on the beach somewhere, standing in the surf, the sun at their backs. She gingerly reinserted the photo and then found his driver's license. Johnson was his last name.

In the search bar of her cellphone's browser, she typed in Brett and Carolina Johnson. The news story that popped up on the screen got Tatiana's blood pumping so loud it blocked her hearing. She read the entire story—the last line several times. Clearing the search history on her cellphone, Tatiana sat there as disbelief turned to dismay.

18

Tatiana tiptoed into the bedroom and put Brett's wallet back in his pocket. Then she stood watching him sleep and felt the burn of shame about her earlier conclusions—thinking he had led a privileged life of ease, when the truth was so much different. Holding her breath, she approached his side of the bed and gingerly lifted the covers from his left side. Peering closely, grateful for the moonlight streaming in, she spotted the telltale scar.

How she wanted to wrap her arms around him, soothe him, tell him that she wouldn't leave him. But the truth was, she had to. She couldn't expose him to Vargas.

Tatiana quietly pulled open drawers until she found a change of clothes. She got dressed, then extracted her gun from her holster. Placing the weapon, her ICE badge and wallet on the dresser, she left the room, gently easing the door closed.

She found some instant coffee in the kitchen cupboard. Filling a glass with tap water, she spooned two heaping spoons of coffee into it, stirred and downed it all at once, grimacing as she rummaged through the kitchen drawers for pen and paper.

Sitting down at the table, she wrote:

Brett, thank you for everything. I need to go find Gisella now and bring her home. *I appreciate you wanted to go—more than you'll ever know—but I don't want to put you in danger. Please keep my stuff safe. I trust you.*

Tatiana read the note and thought how it really didn't say what she wanted to say. *Hijole,* Tati, she whispered to herself as she closed her eyes tight to discourage the tears that threatened to spill onto the page. Taking a deep breath, she resumed writing. *When I come back, I want you to teach me how to surf.* Tatiana stared at the page and then quickly scribbled, *Yours, Tati*

That done, she dialed a number on her cellphone. "I need a big favor— actually two big favors."

"Long time, *mi amor.* Don't I get an *hola?*"

"*Bueno, hola,* Rodrigo. I don't have a lot of time. I need to get to Cabo San Lucas. And I need some cash, a burner phone, a passport, and a gun when I get there."

"And you come to me."

"I can't get to my funds right now, but you know I'm good for it." Tatiana thought for a moment. "Make me a Canadian this time."

"It's two o'clock in the morning, *mujer.* This is going to cost you extra."

"Fine. I also need a ride."

Rodrigo sighed. "Where are you?"

"I'll meet you on Camino Real at the 7-Eleven there."

"Thirty minutes okay?"

"It'll have to do," said Tatiana.

With the note she wrote to Brett, Tatiana went to the door of the bedroom and slid it and her cellphone underneath. She put her hand on the door and listened to steady breathing. The same at the doorway of Chico and Rosalie. She silently wished them a safe passage.

Then she slipped out of the house and walked down the street to the 7-Eleven.

Rodrigo's truck was already in the parking lot when she arrived. He turned off his bright lights and got out.

"Nice to see you, *bonita!*" he grinned, exposing a missing front tooth.

"You, too, Rodrigo."

"Say it like you mean it, *mujer*."

"Actually, I do mean it. This time. Okay, time for business."

Rodrigo chuckled and then frowned, pulling a brown paper bag out of his pocket and handing it to her. "Like I said on the phone, you might be *guapa*, but this don't come cheap."

Tatiana opened the bag and peered inside. She flipped open the passport that lay on top of a pile of cash. Her photo with the name Felicia Torez. "I'll pay," she said. "I always do."

"There's two grand in there. All I could collect this fast. And here's the burner." Rodrigo handed her a cellphone.

"Come on, get in. There's a bus leaving soon that will get you through the border to Tijuana. Then you've got a direct flight to Cabo."

Tatiana went around to the passenger door and slammed it shut as he revved the engine. Before long they were heading down the nearly empty street.

"Business good?" Tatiana asked.

"*Esta bien*. You win some, you lose some."

"Like your tooth?"

"How was I supposed to know the *bonita* at the bar had a boyfriend?"

Tatiana laughed. "Maybe ask?"

She had known Rodrigo for at least a decade, since her days at the Huntington PD. Every time she saw him, there'd been a recent altercation over a woman. Never mind that he had a long-time, live-in girlfriend.

"How's Monica?"

"The same. She shops, she cooks, she complains."

Tatiana glanced over at Rodrigo, whose belly had enlarged since the last time she'd seen him. She thought about commenting on Monica's cooking ability, but bit her tongue.

"What about you, *mujer*? Any *hombre* in your life? Or do I still have a chance?"

Brett flashed through Tatiana's mind, and she felt a warm rush.

"*Hijole*! I'm too late. You wound me!" he cried.

"Please keep your eyes on the road," Tatiana said as she took the passport and money out of the bag and slid them into her pocket.

"The piece you ordered will be in Cabo when you arrive. You'll be picked up by Maria Elena."

"Rodrigo, you're hiring women now? I'm impressed."

He snorted. "That wasn't my decision. She's the boss lady's right-hand *chica.*"

Rodrigo pulled into the San Diego bus station, which appeared deserted. Stopping in front of the entrance, he turned to her. "*Que te vaya bien,*" he said, wishing her good luck.

"*Igualmente, Rodrigo, y gracias.*" Tatiana pulled open the truck's door, hopped out and headed for the large double doors.

Once inside, she purchased a one-way ticket to Tijuana. Then she stopped at a vending machine for some snacks. Picking a bag of cheese puffs and a beef jerky stick, she went back outside to wait for her bus. As she snacked on the food, visions of her and Brett in the shower kept flitting across her mind. Each time she saw his face, her heart clenched. She thought about calling him, but what good would that do except make things worse? Besides, she had to focus on finding Gisella right now.

Brett sat up in bed. Tatiana's scent was still in the air. He knew before he glanced at her side of the bed that she was gone. The word fled ran through his mind. He spied the note on the floor in front of the closed door and went over to pick it up.

"Damnit, Tatiana!" He said to the empty room once he finished reading. He balled up the note and threw it into the trash.

19

Abuelita cocooned a six-year-old Tatiana in her shawl as the police officers checked the apartment.

"Why didn't you tell me, *nietita*?"

"You're the child's grandmother?" A lady police officer asked.

"*Sí*. I am. Rosa Romero."

"And the child's mother is Rina Romero, your daughter?"

"Yes, but *Dios mío*! I had no idea what was going on here."

"The child says she is six years old?"

"That is correct."

"We'll need to talk to you more, *Señora*, about future plans for Tatiana. We've put out an arrest warrant for your daughter for child endangerment and abandonment."

"*Sí, sí, como no*. I will tell you whatever you wish, but can I take the child with me? She's seen enough of this."

"She can be removed from the premises, but she needs to go to the hospital first, for a checkup. You can go with her. We'll have an officer take you there, and you'll meet a social worker. She will most likely need to see your home before the child can be released to you."

An officer approached to take them from the apartment, and her grandmother, still holding Tatiana tight, started to follow him.

"*Abuelita*! I want to get Tessa."

"We need to go now, *niña*."

"Mama gave her to me. I need Tessa."

"Where is Tessa?" asked the officer. "I can get her."

"In my bedroom under the covers. She sleeps with me."

The officer returned with a rag doll that Tatiana grabbed and buried her face in.

Tatiana climbed off the plane in Cabo and made her way to baggage claim, where Rodrigo had instructed her to meet her point of contact. She spied a short, young Mexican woman with a backpack. She had braided, long, black hair coiled on her head like a crown.

Tatiana smiled and the woman smiled back, looking up at Tatiana through thick black bangs.

"Maria Elena?"

The young woman nodded. "*Tio* Rodrigo said you might need a ride to the hacienda."

"That'd be great."

"*Tia* Lupe's car is outside."

When they stepped into the muggy air filled with the smell of jet fuel and smoke, Tatiana coughed.

"It is trash burning day here. It smells better at the hacienda." Maria Elena pointed to a dark green Cadillac in the dirt parking lot. "*Vamanos*."

Once they were on the road, Tatiana flashed on Gisella, and the anxiety that had thrummed at the back of her head since she got the phone call from Macaw became louder. Wrenching her thoughts back to the now, she asked Maria Elena, "How long have you known *Tia* Lupe?"

"About a year. I also brought a friend of mine to live with her."

"Oh, you did. Who is that?"

"Her name is Lena. Now she's apprenticing for *Tia* Lupe to make furniture. I tried, but it's not for me."

"What is for you?"

Maria Elena glanced at Tatiana and then turned her attention back to the road.

"I want to move to the United States and attend Quantico and work for the FBI."

"That's pretty specific. Where'd you come up with that idea?"

"I watch American television—since I was young."

"It's hard work. Television makes it look more exciting than it is."

Maria Elena brushed her bangs out of her eyes and peered at a sign that read Todos Santos.

"I don't expect each day to be a television show."

Brett breathed a sigh of relief when he climbed on his boat. Unlocking the cabin door, he made his way inside and flopped down on the bench seat. He looked at the bag with Tatiana's gun, badge and cellphone in it, and sighed.

In the kitchen, he kneeled in front of the cabinet under his sink, removing the cleaning fluids that sat in front of his small safe. He dialed the code and gingerly placed the items inside. Closing the cabinet door, he stood up. Maybe he could leave his thoughts of Tatiana there with her things and get back to his life now, to his surfing, to some semblance of calm.

When they pulled up to Lupe's hacienda, Tatiana gasped. "Macaw told me this place was beautiful, but I had no idea."

"*Tia* Lupe runs the hacienda by herself. There is no man helping her," stated Maria Elena.

"That's what I heard." Tatiana gathered up her things and opened the Cadillac's door to the sweet scent of jasmine.

"You're right. The air smells amazing here."

"Everything is amazing here," said Maria Elena. "I'll take you to *Tia* Lupe."

They walked through an arched entrance heavy with bright fuchsia bougainvillea and into a breathtaking cobblestone courtyard that smelled of honeysuckle and roses. In the center of the space stood a statue of a woman with long flowing hair, naked breasts and pale curved hips, holding a bucket on her head from which water bubbled and trickled down her stone exterior into a large bowl. Startled by their entrance, a bird stopped bathing in the fountain's bowl and flew away into a nearby olive tree.

"Go ahead and sit down." Maria Elena pointed to a small table with two chairs that sat next to the fountain. "I'll go get *Tia* Lupe."

Tatiana sat and gazed at the fountain. As she watched the water and listened to birds rustling in the trees, she suddenly felt a flattening fatigue. She started to doze off, then heard someone approach and opened her eyes.

"*Disculpame*, I didn't mean to startle you. I am Lupe Sanchez."

Tatiana looked up into the eyes of an older woman with spun silver hair. She wore a smock sprinkled with wood shavings over a blouse and slacks.

"Forgive me for interrupting your work." Tatiana started to stand, but Lupe put out her hand.

"You are exhausted, I can see that. Please stay seated." Lupe sat down and smiled at Tatiana. "I have asked Leticia to bring us some refreshments."

"That would be wonderful," said Tatiana. "Thank you so much for your hospitality. Macaw has told me many great things about you."

"Macaw is a great man. I am blessed every day to know that my niece chose him, and he chose her, of course. But forgive me, you are looking for Ramona Valdez."

It was a statement, not a question, but Tatiana answered anyway, "Yes, and another person, Gisella Reyes, my mentor." The thought of Gisella not being okay tore at Tatiana's heart when she said this.

Lupe studied Tatiana's expression and murmured, "Gisella. She means much to you, no?"

Tatiana swallowed hard, trying to contain her emotions. All she could manage was a nod.

"Gisella is still alive, if that's what concerns you."

Tatiana was shocked, her heart banged against the inside of her ribcage. "How do you know?"

"I will fill you in. But first let me see what's holding up Leticia with our food."

Once Lupe left, Tatiana allowed herself to breathe. Deep slow breaths. She hadn't realized until now how shallowly she'd been breathing. She wished Lupe had stayed to tell her the rest of what she knew about Gisella. Tatiana heard a loud rustle behind her then. She jumped up, reached for the gun that wasn't there, and spun around.

"Is that any way to greet me, Tati?"

20

"Gisella! I don't understand. I thought you were—."

"Being held by Vargas? We needed to make that rumor up for reasons I'll explain. I'm so sorry to have had to do that to you. I know how worried you must have been."

As if propelled by a jet pack, Tatiana rushed to Gisella, grabbing on tight as the older woman embraced her. To Tatiana's horror, she began to sob.

"Shh, *mija*. I'm fine. *Esta bien*." Gisella soothed her. Once Tatiana got herself under control, she leaned back and looked into Gisella's no-nonsense brown eyes.

"You're tired, Tati. And I bet you haven't eaten much, either. There's food coming, and then you should take a nap."

The fatigue weighed on Tatiana so heavily, she had to agree with Gisella. She sat down at the table across from her.

"What a piece of paradise," Gisella commented. A parrot cried out in the distance, and a nearby palm tree swayed in the slight breeze. "Macaw was badly hurt not long ago and recuperated here. I can see why."

At the mention of being hurt, Tatiana flashed on the last time she and Gisella had come up against Vargas. The replay of that night often plagued her. She wished she could wipe it from her mind.

"It's not like last time, *mija*," Gisella said quietly. "We have the advantage this time. He won't see us coming."

A young woman swept into the courtyard just then, carrying a tray filled with several dishes. A bowl full of fresh strawberries with a side of cream, another bowl of salsa, some chips, and tamales with green tomatillo sauce.

Lupe followed behind her.

"I know you told me that you aren't mother and daughter, Gisella, but this beautiful woman looks just like you!"

Tatiana felt warm inside as she dipped a strawberry into the whipped cream.

"The daughter I never had," said Gisella. "Turns out water can be thicker than blood."

"I would agree with that!" Lupe pulled two napkins from the pocket of her workshop apron and placed them on the edge of the table. "Is there anything else you need?"

"This is more than enough," said Gisella.

"Leticia prepared the avocado room on the north end of the hacienda, so you will have shade during the hot part of the day soon to come, Tatiana."

Tatiana looked up at Lupe. "Thank you for everything."

"It is you I should be thanking," said Lupe, who pulled a sprig of jasmine from a nearby vine and put it behind her ear. "I understand it is you who saved dear Chico and Rosalie from Vargas's claws. I owe you a tremendous gratitude for that."

"I was just doing my job."

Lupe raised her eyebrows. "I understand your job is ICE, no? Rather than returning the brother and sister to Mexico to get swallowed up by Vargas, you saved their lives. That is much more than they ever thought possible. I will leave you both to eat and rest."

After scarfing down her food, Tatiana followed Gisella to her room. Its dark green walls cocooned her as she stepped inside. A bed lay against the far wall and a mini bar ran the length of the room on the other side. A fresh hibiscus flower lay on her pillow, and the bedside table contained a carafe of water and a glass.

"There's a shower in the bathroom, as far as I know," said Gisella. "And Lupe has clothing in the bureau that will fit you." She raised her hand to stop Tatiana when she started to speak.

"I know you've got questions. Rest first, before those wheels start spinning. I'll tell you everything when you wake up later."

"I just need a couple of hours, and then I'm ready to go."

Gisella turned and left the room, shutting the door firmly behind her.

Tatiana looked at the bed and decided to lie down for a while and then take a shower. She peeled off her clothing and slid between the cool sheets, sighing when her body sunk into the velvet-soft mattress. Just a couple of hours, she told herself as she drifted off.

Brett stood and stretched his back and neck—both felt as stiff as his surfboard. He'd been writing for a good two hours. He went out on deck and stretched out the back of his legs. This was the only thing he didn't like about working on the boat. It was so cramped. But he couldn't go back to the house yet. The real estate agent he'd hired to watch over the mansion was baffled at why he didn't just rent it out. He never answered the question, so she stopped asking.

His biggest frustration right now was that he hadn't surfed in days. The last time he'd gone this long without getting into the water was after the incident. Tomorrow morning, for sure, he'd get some surfing in.

As he headed back into the cabin, Brett spotted a man standing on the dock a few boats away, staring at him. When they made eye contact, the man turned around and began walking away, looking back once. Most likely Brett was just being paranoid after the events of the last few days. He went inside to make lunch.

21

When Tatiana awoke a few hours later in the dark room, she blinked, confused by her surroundings. Then it registered where she was. She stared up at the ceiling and watched the fan circle. Her mind suddenly filled with thoughts of Brett.

She wondered if he was relieved to get back to his life. A life that might even include a girlfriend. Tatiana had been so wrapped up in her own agenda that it never crossed her mind that Brett might be involved with someone else.

She needed to clear her head. A shower would help. Getting up from the bed, she headed for the shower that promised to rinse away all thoughts of Brett.

Brett decided to go to bed early. He set his alarm clock for three in the morning. He wanted to get to the beach in plenty of time before sunrise. He loved to be in the ocean when the sun sent its first rays into the horizon. The air became crisper as the seagulls awoke, announcing with their first cries that they were ready to scavenge for their morning meals of sand crabs and fish.

By then, Brett would be sitting on his surfboard, the ocean rocking him up and down as he waited for a wave. He could always tell when a good one was coming, even before he spotted the wave. It would show in the distance, swelling and building momentum. When it was yards away, he'd get up on his knees, ready to jump up and ride the wave to shore. Something about repeating the process soothed and even washed Brett's soul.

Tatiana found Gisella sitting at the bistro table in the courtyard eating something that smelled incredibly delicious.

"Thank you for letting me sleep."

"It was either that or watch you fall over somewhere. Have a seat. Leticia will bring you some of Lupe's famous *Arroz con Pollo*."

Tatiana pulled up a chair and sat down, thinking how Gisella always seemed to read her mind and anticipate what she needed next.

"Any word on Ramona?"

"Word is she's being held in a hilltop mansion outside of Cabo. We've only gotten one spotty communication from her. Enough to know she's alive, but that's it. We're trying to figure out how to best proceed. We can't just go busting in. The man who owns the home is a three-percenter here."

"Three-percenter?"

"One of the elites, in terms of money. The wealth holders here are the power players. Even more well-defined than in the States. The man holding Ramona is Russian, and a top dog in their syndicate. Local law enforcement is most likely in his pocket, and word is he's in cahoots with Vargas. We spread the rumor that Vargas had me, trying to get some reaction from the Russian. The hope was that if he thought Vargas might be holding a member of the FBI, he'd go see Vargas, leaving us some room to get in and extract Ramona. We've been sitting on the house for a while now, though, and the guy never leaves. This is all a real mess. One that could get me canned." Gisella let out an uncharacteristic sigh.

Tatiana studied her mentor's face, noting telltale worry lines making their way around her eyes. If Gisella was concerned about losing her job, there was cause for concern. Tatiana knew the job was all Gisella really had.

Leticia bustled into the courtyard and set a steaming bowl of *Arroz con Pollo* in front of Tatiana. "A soda to drink, *Senorita* Tatiana? Or some *té, café?*"

"Black tea would be wonderful, *muchas gracias*." Tatiana inhaled the aroma of chicken, onion and garlic wafting up at her.

When Leticia was out of earshot, Gisella continued. "We were going to send in an agent as a maid—the owner of the mansion put out a request yesterday to a local agency—but she's been detained by another case. I can't go in. I'm too old. He apparently likes them young and pretty."

Tatiana put down the spoonful of broth and rice she'd been about to devour. "Let me. I can go in."

Gisella shook her head vigorously. "That's impossible, Tati. You're ICE now. And besides, you said that person you detained at the beach gave you the message from Vargas."

"He was probably told to just say it to whatever border agent was there. Besides, I look totally different out of uniform. I'm the right age, and I'm Mexican. I'm perfect for this."

"Even if you're right about them not knowing it's you, what about your job?"

"I'm still a law enforcement officer. Just consider this a joint task force operation."

"A totally unsanctioned one," said Gisella. "None of our superiors would be okay with shoot first and ask questions later."

"If you bring Ramona back, I don't think they'd care how it was done."

Gisella looked into Tatiana's eyes. She could see her mentor weighing the request, but she shook her head. "No. I appreciate it, but I can't risk anything happening to you."

"You prepared me for this assignment. I want to do this. For you."

Gisella looked at the fountain. Tatiana waited.

Finally, Gisella said in a low voice, "If I decide to let you do this, you're going to have to breathe, *mija*."

22

Gisella stayed on the phone a long time with her FBI associates discussing Tatiana going into the mansion to extract Ramona. After a while, Tatiana began to think it was a no go. But then Gisella returned to the courtyard and announced, "Okay, you're going in this evening." She stopped talking and a look crossed her face that Tatiana had never seen before.

"I'm not going to lie to you. This man is a monster. We can't send you in with a wire or anything. He does a sweep of all employees regularly. Your contact will be the groundskeeper, Ernesto. He's FBI and passes us written notes at the back of the property. You need to say something about bougainvillea when you meet Ramona, so she knows you're one of us. If you feel like your life is in imminent danger, the emergency code word is rhododendron."

Gisella studied Tatiana's face. "I know you can do this. Maria Elena will tell you all about the layout of the mansion and more about our Russian friend. And we've got someone coming in soon with your wardrobe."

"Maria Elena has been to the mansion?"

"She was being held at the mansion. Not sure if you've figured this out, but Lupe is more than a woodworker. She's a *Coyote de Dios*. This hacienda is part of an underground railroad system for helping trafficking victims escape. Many of them change their identities and move on to other regions of Mexico or South America and sometimes the US, like Rosalie and Chico. In exchange, they're required to offer information about the trafficking network. In addition to getting intel on the cartel, Ramona has been working behind-the-scenes with Lupe to help the victims."

"That explains what Chico told me about Ramona helping him."

"Lupe has some backers here in Mexico and the States. They're mostly well-off people appalled by what's happening. Fortunately, a lot of those players have muscle, which means this place is protected. I can't say that for the house you're going to, though."

"What do you know about Ramona?" Tatiana asked.

"She's been deep undercover for seven years now. From what we can tell, her cover still hasn't been blown. But she's obviously being held against her will. She likely has enough intel to blow this trafficking ring wide open, so we need to get her out."

Maria Elena approached, and Gisella greeted her. "*Buenas tardes.* Tell Tatiana anything she needs to know. I have some calls to make."

"Thanks for talking to me. How about we sit down?" Tatiana said to the girl. Once Maria Elena was seated across from her, Tatiana put her elbows on the bistro table and leaned in slightly. Maria Elena flinched, but held steady.

"I know this is difficult, but can you tell me about the mansion?"

Maria Elena's brown eyes clouded, but she nodded, her chin taking on a firm resolve. She spent the next twenty minutes describing the layout of the mansion and grounds, and the proclivities of the owner.

"If he likes you, then you have to..." Maria Elena took in a deep breath and sat up straighter. "If he likes you, you must go to him at night. He has you do awful things, and sometimes you are beaten."

Tatiana's stomach roiled, but she leaned hard on her training, willing herself to remain objective and observant. She had to ask as many questions as possible while she had the chance.

"How many girls does he have at once?"

Maria Elena looked at Tatiana, her eyes hard. Tatiana recognized that look. Better to push the pain back, so the anger, which was safer, came forward.

"He usually has at least two, but sometimes just one. And he also has men."

"Is there any point where there's vulnerability? Where he could be overpowered? Is he alone in the room when others are in there with him? Or, are there guards in there, too?"

"Guards stand outside the door, but they can come in at a moment's notice," said Maria Elena. "He has to give the word, though."

"What's the word, and did that ever happen when you were there?"

A look of horror and pain clouded Maria Elena's eyes. "There was a young boy who didn't want to, you know."

"Tell me about that time, please."

"He screamed and started to fight the man, and then he bit him. Maria Elena's face crumpled, and tears spilled down the sides of her cheeks.

"The man called out, *ven guardia*, and the guard came in and pulled the boy off him and..." Maria Elena trailed off.

Tatiana waited in silence, focusing on the fountain bubbling next to them.

Maria Elena resolutely wiped the tears from the sides of her eyes and continued. "The man told him to finish off the boy, so he shot him in the head in front of us. And then the man kept going like nothing happened."

"I'm so sorry you had to experience that," Tatiana said quietly. "Just one more question. Does the man drink anything or take drugs during these nights?"

"No drugs, but he does drink."

"Do you know what he drinks?"

"It smells like whiskey."

Tatiana sat forward and gently put her hand on Maria Elena's clenched ones. "I know that was hard for you, but it will help us stop him. Thank you."

"I must go now to see if *Tia* Lupe needs me," said Maria Elena.

Once she had walked away, Gisella appeared seemingly out of nowhere like she always did. "Good job, *mija*. You're a natural for this. You sure you want to stay with ICE?"

"I don't know," Tatiana admitted. "I'm rethinking everything about my life right now."

Gisella raised her eyebrow. "Everything?"

Brett flashed through Tatiana's mind, and she squirmed under Gisella's gaze.

"It's the surfer, isn't it?"

"You don't want to hear about that. It's not *importante*."

"There's more to life than work. Take it from me."

"I thought you loved your work?"

"I do, but there is more. You figure that out—sometimes too late. You love him, *mija*? I can see that. It's okay. I had a love like that once."

"Had? What happened?"

"He didn't make it."

"Didn't make it? Like died?"

"No, he didn't make it like not being able to handle me and what I do. He wanted a woman who stayed home and raised the kids and made the dinner."

"Oh, sorry." Tatiana didn't know what to say to that.

"But this man. He doesn't seem like that."

"He offered to come with me here."

"So why didn't he?"

"He's a surfer, not an agent. I didn't want him getting hurt on my conscience. That's all," said Tatiana.

"Or maybe you didn't want to hurt him?"

"I ruin things Gisella," Tatiana blurted out. "I hurt people. They leave."

"Ah, *mija*. You don't hurt anyone. You're talking about your mother. But she left because she had a problem. It had nothing to do with you."

Tatiana started to speak, but Gisella's cellphone rang. She held up her finger and answered.

When she hung up a minute later, the look on her face told Tatiana the conversation was going to have to wait.

"Your wardrobe is here. We need to get you to the mansion right away. Word is the Russian may finally be leaving the house and flying out of the country on business. So, you need to get in and get Ramona out ASAP."

"After talking to Maria Elena, I've got an idea for that."

Gisella's eyes brightened. "Tell me."

23

Dressed in a maid's outfit and wedge heels that really pissed her off, Tatiana stomped out of her room and into the courtyard for Gisella to see.

"Woohoo!" Gisella grinned as Tatiana pulled up on the front of the tight-fitting top with one hand and down on her short skirt with the other.

"Take a good look, because you're never going to see me dressed like this again," Tatiana retorted.

"Better that than the smelly bag lady outfits we had to wear on that one op, remember?"

Tatiana's nose wrinkled as she recalled the disgusting cocktail of garbage and urine they'd sprayed on themselves.

Gisella rose from her seat and checked the watch on her arm. "Time to get this show on the road. Your carriage awaits. A van from the agency."

Trying to stay strong and impartial, Tatiana thought about hugging Gisella, but decided against it.

"*Brazos* are okay, *mija*. It's not like anyone is going to watch you hug me," said Gisella, who took Tatiana into her arms and patted her back reassuringly.

They pulled apart and made their way outside, where Tatiana climbed into the back of a van that read Lindra on the side. Sitting back as comfortably as she could, she set a small, plastic bag beside her. Inside was a change of clothing and a toiletry bag containing a toothbrush, toothpaste and hairbrush. She looked the part of an orphan and getting into character would be easy.

"Chica! So good to see you. Is *abuelita* here?" Tatiana's mother stood on the front porch with a man she'd never seen before. It was always a different man each time she visited, which was about once a year since Tatiana had come to live with her grandmother. This one leered at Tatiana, making her skin crawl.

Her mother strode into her grandmother's living room, her boyfriend following. "What are you now, in college?"

"I'm a junior in high school."

"Oh, good, I didn't miss the graduation!" Her mother laughed, gazing up adoringly at the creep, who couldn't keep his eyes off Tatiana's breasts.

"Abuelita isn't here, but she'll be back soon. I don't think she wants you here when she's gone."

"Que estúpido," her mother exclaimed, plopping herself down on the couch and throwing her shopping bag-sized purse on the floor next to her. Tatiana eyed the bag, knowing that her mother likely planned to pilfer from the house if she didn't keep an eye on her.

Flinging her black hair over one shoulder, her mother eyed Tatiana and asked, "Since when can't a woman come visit her own mother and daughter? How about a *cerveza* for me and my friend? Oh, sorry, rude me. His name is Paulo."

"Mucho gusto," Paulo said, smirking at Tatiana.

"We don't have any alcohol." Tatiana remained standing in the room as Paulo sat down next to her mother.

Tatiana's mother laughed, but her eyes hardened. *"Mentiras,* Tatiana. I know that *abuelita* keeps a stash of tequila in the cupboard by the washing machine." She got up and stalked to the kitchen.

"I'm not telling lies." Tatiana kept one eye trained on Paulo and one eye on her mother as she riffled in the kitchen cabinets. "Try the Drano," she mumbled under her breath.

Her mother called out, "What did you say?"

"I said there's nothing in that cabinet but Drano, Rina."

"Don't call me Rina. I'm mama to you." Clearly agitated about not finding anything to drink, her mother came back into the living room and demanded, "Tell me where her stash is, or I'll—"

"What? Leave?"

Apparently done with the drama, Paulo rose from the couch. "Let's go. You can have your family reunion another time."

About to protest, Rina closed her mouth and picked up her purse, sliding her arm through Paulo's. "Tell your *abuelita* I said hi."

When the door closed behind them and Tatiana heard the old jalopy head away from the house, she looked down at her hands to see they were shaking.

They pulled up to the mansion after climbing a long driveway. The van headed under a giant granite archway, then stopped in front of a massive front door.

The driver didn't say anything as Tatiana gathered up her small bag and pulled the van door open, stepping onto a stone driveway. She slid the door shut and looked up at a staircase leading to a red door. At the top, she tapped the door with a heavy brass knocker.

A maid opened the door. Her eyes glanced at Tatiana, then darted to the floor. "*Ven*," she squeaked, indicating that Tatiana should enter.

"Is that the new maid?" said a woman's voice from the other room.

"*Sí, Señora* Ramona."

"I'll be right out."

The maid scuttled off, and Tatiana waited.

Moments later, Tatiana smelled expensive perfume and Ramona

wiggled in, filling the foyer with her presence. She wore a low-cut velvet burgundy dress and dangling diamond earrings.

"What's your name, dear?" she asked.

"Felicia. I come from Lindra."

"Wonderful," said Ramona, coming closer slowly. I am *Señora* Ramona. I require a maid to assist me with my wardrobe. That would be you."

Tatiana gave her a small smile.

"I trust you have worked as a personal maid?"

"*Sí, Señora*, and in the house, too."

The maid who had answered the door walked by with a vase of flowers and set it on a table in the foyer where they stood.

"Beautiful, Gloria, thank you," said Ramona.

"As a house maid, I would create bouquets made of bougainvillea," said Tatiana. She noted a spark in Ramona's eyes when she said this.

"What a wonderful idea. Come, I will take you to my wardrobe now. We can start with a good clean out of the closet."

"*Sí, Señora* Ramona."

Tatiana followed her to the third floor, where they walked along a hallway filled with plush gold carpeting. Ramona opened a door and stepped inside, indicating for Tatiana to follow.

"Before my closet, I require some quick seamstress work. Let's go in the bathroom, and I'll show you."

Ramona headed to the bathroom, and Tatiana followed. Closing the door behind them, Ramona swung around to face her new assistant and waited, her eyes trained on Tatiana's face.

"Ramona, I'm so glad to see you are okay. There are many people concerned."

"People such as?" Ramona asked, warily.

"Gisella and Macaw."

She visibly relaxed at the mention of their names. "Go on."

"I am Tatiana Romero," she spoke quietly. "Formally ICE, but I'm participating in a joint operation with the FBI."

"Thank God," said Ramona as she eased herself down onto a plush chair in front of a vanity. "I've got all we need to sink him with Interpol. It's time to get out of here."

"They sent me in here with a plan, but only you know the lay of the land here, so—"

They heard someone entering the bedroom then. Tatiana grabbed a needle and thread from the bureau and began threading it. She pretended to look up surprised when the bathroom door swung open. An Adonis of a man with brittle gray eyes stood there. Mid-forties with a lean, yet muscular build and full head of blond hair, he wore a charcoal dress shirt and black dress pants.

"There you are. I was wondering where you'd gone off to," he said in a Russian accent.

"Andrej, darling. I have the new maid darning a hole for me."

He noted the needle and thread in Tatiana's hands. "That appears to be the wrong color," he said as Tatiana pushed black thread through the eye of the needle.

Ramona reached out a hand adorned with long, lacquered burgundy nails and brushed the man's cheek. "Darling, this is for the zipper in the back, which is loose and black. Why don't you go down to supper? I'll be right there."

Andrej's gaze rested then on Tatiana. "A new girl?"

Tatiana kept her eyes trained on the floor, but Andrej reached out and tipped up her chin, forcing her to meet his gaze.

"Good choice, my dear," he said approvingly, now taking ahold of Tatiana's shoulders and turning her around. "Did you have her checked for contraband?"

"Yes, of course I had her checked. The poor waif has nothing more than the clothing on her back. Let's go have something to eat, *mi amor*."

"What about your dress?"

"Easier access for you," she practicality purred as she led him out of the room. "Felicia, dear, reorganize my closet while I'm gone."

"*Sí, Señora* Ramona."

Tatiana waited until the door closed, then sat down in front of

Ramona's vanity. Picking up her things, she reached in and extracted her small toiletry kit. She felt inside of the lining. It was still there.

24

Brett stood in his kitchen eating a banana while his coffee brewed. The best surfing this morning was supposed to be at the border. Where he and Tatiana had met.

Where was she and what was she doing? Thoughts of their time in the shower filled Brett with a mixture of desire and a need to ensure her safety. Several years of therapy had taught him that he couldn't do anything about either of those instincts. Tatiana had left without him. He had to face that fact and believe her words, "I'm coming back." Therapy had also taught him that healthy distractions were the best cure, which is how surfing had become his lifeline.

The coffee finished brewing, Brett took some half and half out of the fridge and poured it into the coffee. He took a long drink. It was still dark out. Good. He would be able to see the sunrise.

When Brett pulled into the Imperial Beach parking lot twenty minutes later, the sky had turned from black to a pale gray. He got out of the van and put his keys under the front seat. Grabbing his surfboard and a towel, he headed toward the sound of the waves. When the water hit his toes, Brett smiled. Setting down his surfboard, he sat next to it. He'd wait until the sun peeked out of the horizon, then get in the water and ride the first waves of the day.

As he waited, Brett focused on the sound of the waves rolling in and receding. Just as the next wave came in and ocean water covered his feet, Brett sensed someone behind him. He started to stand up, but a man's arm encircled his neck in a steely grip.

"Where is she?" The voice in his ear had a Mexican accent. The arm loosened, freeing his windpipe, so Brett could speak.

"Who?"

"Your girlfriend. Where is she? The ICE agent."

"I don't know."

The arm tightened around Brett's neck again. He grappled to free himself from the vice grip but began to feel faint from lack of airflow.

"You do know, and you better tell me, or you're dead." The man's breath smelled of garlic and beer.

"She left. I have no idea where."

Brett could feel anger tightening up the man's body. He braced himself for another round of intense choking.

Just then a light flashed from the parking lot. Brett felt the man turn his head in that direction. He let go of Brett's throat and yelled. "I'll be back, gringo. Figure out where your girlfriend went by the time I come back, or I'll start removing fingers."

Brett landed face-first in the surf, sputtering as ocean water made its way into his mouth. When he surfaced, the man was gone, and Brett could see the outlines of two surfers and their boards coming toward him on the sand. Brett lunged toward shore and grabbed his surfboard, then began making his way in their direction.

One of the surfers commented when he walked within earshot, "Hey man. We thought we were gonna be the first ones."

Brett started to speak but stopped to cough, his throat feeling raw.

"You okay?" One of them asked.

"Yeah, almost swallowed that last wave," Brett managed to say.

"Sorry about that, dude. We're supposed to have some killer waves today."

The word killer kicked Brett's anxiety up one-hundred-fold. "Thanks, man. Have a good ride." He ran up the sandy embankment to his van. He had to warn Tatiana, and her cellphone was going to help him find her.

Tatiana awoke in the tiny room—more like a broom closet—that she'd been sent to last night. Faint rays of sunlight slid from underneath the lone window in the room to signify the start of the day. She pulled up the small window shade, wondering when she was supposed to be up for the day. It looked like Ramona was officially her boss, and she hadn't been given any instructions—except for organizing her closet, which Tatiana had done. She'd been stunned at the magnitude of the clothing Ramona had. An outfit for any occasion imaginable. Even though Ramona's cover in Mexico was as a boutique owner, Tatiana had never seen that much clothing stuffed into one closet.

As the sun's rays grew stronger, Tatiana thought of Brett. Was he surfing? She would love to be there with him right now, watching the sunrise together and stepping into the ocean. She pictured doing so hand-in-hand, and the thought made her feel like her heart was crying.

A loud rap on the door startled her back to reality. She sat up and pulled the covers to her chin as the door swung open. She'd been chagrined to discover the night before that her door had no locks—as did none of the other doors she'd encountered.

Ramona came inside and quietly shut the door behind her. She smelled of whiskey and sweat, and her face was streaked with mascara tears.

Taken aback, Tatiana made room for Ramona to sit on the side of the bed.

"What happened?"

With shaking hands, Ramona pushed her long mane of black, silky hair off her shoulders, exposing bruises on her upper arms.

Tatiana sucked in a deep breath. *"Dios mío*, Ramona!"

"Andrej had one of his nights, and I was the object of his affection," she said wryly. She then winced and held her side.

"Your ribs? Did he break them?"

She nodded. "I'll have one of the maids bandage me up." Ramona's pain was visible in her eyes.

"Did he pass out?"

"Yes, but he usually doesn't stay down for long. Tell me your plan."

"I've got some ketamine. Enough to put down him and his men so that the FBI can get in. We just need to get them to ingest it."

"We can do that. I've got an in with the cook, and she is motivated. Andrej raped her niece, and she's never been the same."

Ramona's demeanor changed as she eyed Tatiana. "I'm going to need you to keep me under control with this. I—" she stopped herself and winced again, her brown eyes clouding with venom. "Stop me from giving that disgusting pig of a man all of the ketamine and then stabbing his eyes out. I have never hated someone so much in my life."

"Going to sleep and never waking up is much too kind a fate for him," said Tatiana.

Ramona nodded. "There is also one guard who will help us. Antonio, the son of the cook."

"Good. Tonight, do you think we can—"

Tatiana was interrupted by Andrej bellowing in the hall.

"Ramona, where are you? Get out here now, or I'll teach you another lesson!"

25

Ramona put her finger to her lips, warning Tatiana to be quiet. Bracing herself to stand, she grimaced as she pushed up from Tatiana's bed and exited her room.

"There you are! Where in the hell were you?"

"I thought I would freshen up," said Ramona. "Why don't you go back and lie down? It's still early."

"I can lie down when I'm dead. Isn't that what the Americans say?"

"That's what they say, Andrej."

"Oh, now it's Andrej! What happened to darling? Were things a little rough for you last night? If you would just behave, I wouldn't have to teach you such lessons."

"How about some breakfast? We can eat in your room. I'll have the cook bring up a tray."

"Make it quick," he snarled. "And then get back in here." Tatiana heard the door slam, and seconds later Ramona stepped back into her room, her hand extended.

Tatiana reached for her toiletry bag and slid her fingers into the lining, pulling out a small plastic bag containing white powder. She pressed it into Ramona's hand as she whispered, "I'll meet you in the kitchen."

Brett peeled into the marina parking lot and hopped out of the van, running to his boat. Once inside the cabin, he got Tatiana's cellphone out of the safe and powered it on. He pressed the last number she had called.

A man's sleepy voice came on the line after just one ring. "Tatiana, *mi amor*, your excursion over so quickly?"

"This isn't Tatiana, buddy," said Brett, irritated at the jealousy that swept through him.

The voice woke up quickly. "Who is this?"

"A friend of Tatiana's. Who's this?"

"You her *novio*? Look, *amigo*, I don't need any more broken teeth. This is just business with her."

Her boyfriend. That stopped Brett for a second.

"Hello?"

"Yeah, this is her boyfriend," Brett said. "She's in danger. I need to get to her fast."

"How do I know you aren't the enemy?" Brett could tell the man was now concerned he'd spoken too soon.

"Only a boyfriend would know her well, right?"

"Okay."

"Tatiana is hotheaded and beautiful and infuriating and does whatever she wants whenever she wants—never mind how it affects other people. But she's fair, and she wants justice, and for all her faults, she has a big heart that she doesn't show to many people. And then there's that dry sense of humor."

There was silence on the other end of the line, then Brett heard a chuckle. "Okay, all I know is that she went to a hacienda outside of Cabo. I don't know where it's at, but the woman who owns it is named Lupe Sanchez, and she's a woodworker. Bring Tatiana back safely. She owes me 2 grand."

Tatiana dressed quickly, then headed downstairs toward the smell of breakfast. Stopping in front of the swinging double doors to the kitchen, she heard Ramona's voice. She pushed open the doors and peeked inside.

Ramona and the cook looked up, the wariness in their eyes disappearing when they saw her.

"This is Lisette," Ramona said, "the cook. We were just talking about the special menu for tonight. Antonio will be on duty with another guard."

Tatiana started to speak but hesitated.

"It's okay. I swept the kitchen. It's not bugged," said Ramona.

"I was told of a groundskeeper. Ernesto. Where would I find him?" Tatiana eyed the steaming plate of what looked like huevos rancheros on the marble kitchen island.

Ramona's eyebrows shot up. "Ernesto works in the back most of the time. He tried to speak with me once, but Andrej almost shot him for it. Is he how they found me?"

"Yes, he's FBI."

The relief that swept through Ramona's body was visible. Her usual grand dame demeanor morphed completely as tears moistened her eyes. "That explains some things." Ramona pulled out a chair for herself from a nearby table, wincing visibly when she sat down.

"*Ay, que animale,*" Lisette hissed. "I will get you some aspirin."

As the cook hurried off, Ramona picked up an icepack sitting on the counter and gently placed it on the side of her face. She looked up at Tatiana.

"Ramona, I am so sorry. This must be so hard for you."

"I'll be okay now that I'm going to get out of here," she said. "You have a lovely complexion. And your hair is quite gorgeous. Your mother is Mexican?"

Tatiana nodded. "Was."

"Oh, I'm sorry. My mother is gone, as well. She was quite a fashionista, my mother. Thanks to her, I have my love for fashion. The clothing boutique was my cover, but so much more—it has kept me sane. My second career once I retire from the agency."

"Will you retire after this case?"

"I don't know if I'm up for another case like this one. Hector was a thug—but he would never hurt women or children. This one..." she trailed off.

"I saw Hector's execution," Tatiana said quietly.

Ramona's eyes widened. "You did? At the beach?"

"You seemed to genuinely care for him."

"That wasn't supposed to happen, but yes, I did. He never hurt me. He actually adored me." Ramona gestured toward the eggs. "Go ahead and serve yourself some breakfast. There are plates in the cupboard over there."

"Oh, thank you. Do you want some?"

"No, I'll eat in a while."

Tatiana opened the nearby cupboard and took out a small white plate. She picked up a spoon next to the egg dish and stuck it in, inhaling in appreciation as the scent of onion, cheese and chili pepper wafted out.

"I can't remember the last time I ate a full meal," Tatiana commented.

"That happens when you're deep undercover," Ramona mused, almost to herself. "You lose track of a lot of things, including yourself. You find yourself doing and saying things that you never thought you would do or say. And you find yourself in seeming allegiance with horrible, vile people."

Tatiana had a mouthful of eggs but didn't know how to respond to that one anyway.

"How is Macaw, by the way?"

Tatiana swallowed. "He's doing great. Deep into something with Alexa in South America."

"Alexa is a lucky woman. Now Macaw is a *real* man."

Tatiana nodded, immediately flashing to Brett. Would he ever talk to her again, she wondered?

Ramona sat in silence while Tatiana wolfed down her eggs.

"Oh, good, you ate," commented Lisette when she returned with the aspirin and handed it to Ramona, along with a glass of water.

"*Gracias*, Lisette." Ramona took the aspirin and then set the glass and icepack on the counter. "I better get back to prince charming. You know what to do tonight."

"Know what to do tonight about what?" asked Andrej, who stood in the doorway. He wore the same clothing as the night before.

Ramona quickly rose and sashayed her way toward him.

"Darling, that was supposed to be a surprise! Lisette will be serving your favorite tonight. Borscht. I thought you had a meeting?"

"I do, and I want you present at the meeting to take notes."

"Of course." Ramona soothed, rubbing her hand against his arm. "It's getting late. Let's go to the dining room. Lisette can serve us breakfast there."

Andrej turned to walk out with Ramona, but then swung around and looked directly at Tatiana. "What is your new maid doing in here? What are you hens talking about?"

"Nothing, darling. The poor girl hadn't eaten in hours, so I told her to come into the kitchen for a bit of food before I have her start work for the day. Let's go sit down so we can eat. I'm famished, and I bet you are, too."

Andrej pulled his arm from Ramona's. "Don't tell me what I am," he barked. "Get over here," he called out to Tatiana.

Her throat dropping into her stomach, Tatiana approached, keeping her eyes on the floor.

"Look at me when I'm talking to you," he said, his thumb and forefinger grabbing her chin in a steel grip that hurt. Tatiana willed herself not to flinch.

He squinted at Tatiana as Ramona reached out for Andrej's arm. "Darling, let's go get some food."

Andrej gave Ramona a strong push with one arm that sent her reeling into the kitchen island. "I want this girl in my room this evening. Alone." He let go of Tatiana's chin and grinned. "We'll have some fun."

As he turned to stalk out of the kitchen, he called out to Lisette, "Bring breakfast to my room, and make the coffee black and hot, or you'll be wearing it. Ramona, get yourself cleaned up and hide those bruises. You look terrible."

26

"We'll have him passed out on enough ketamine to flatten a bull before he touches you," Ramona said once it was clear Andrej was out of earshot. "His meeting should last at least an hour. Take the opportunity to talk to Ernesto."

After Ramona made her exit, Lisette crossed herself. "*Gracias a Dios* this will soon be over. And my Graciela will be avenged for what he did to her."

"I'm so sorry to hear about your niece," said Tatiana.

"*Gracias* to you. If you hadn't come, we would be living this same bad dream forever. I better get the man's coffee and breakfast ready. You can go out the kitchen door to find Ernesto. There is a garden shed out back."

Tatiana stepped through the back door into a verdant garden filled with plantings of bird of paradise and hoya, whose waxy flowers emitted a faint floral scent as she passed. She made her way down a carefully tended path, marveling at the juxtaposition of such a lovely garden and such a vile owner. When she neared the back fence, the smell of jasmine perfumed the air, and she remembered an afternoon many years ago.

"*Nietita*, what are you doing?"

Tatiana was in a garden surrounded by jasmine vines she had cut from the largest vine in the yard. Carefully, so as not to knock off the flowers, she had braided two jasmine crowns.

"A *corona* for me and you?" asked her grandmother of the eight-year-old.

"No, for me and Mama," Tatiana replied.

"Oh, I see. *Lo siento, nietita*, but Mama called. She won't be able to visit today."

Disappointment flooded through Tatiana, who suddenly felt like cutting the *coronas* into tiny bits and throwing them away.

"But I myself have always wanted a *corona* made of jasmine *hermosa!*" her grandmother exclaimed. "Can I wear one, *por favor?*"

Tatiana handed her grandmother one of the crowns.

"We must put the crowns on together at the same time, *nietita*! It is very important. Ready? *Uno, dos, tres!*"

She and her grandmother crowned themselves, the heady scent of jasmine filling the air.

"And now, the queen and princess must have tea. A very special tea made of hibiscus flowers."

Tatiana clapped her hands. "*Con galletas chocolate, por favor?*"

"Of course, we must have chocolate cookies!" Her grandmother took her hand as they walked into the kitchen to prepare a royal tea for two.

Tatiana found Ernesto raking out a flower bed. He looked up as she approached, question marks in his eyes.

"*Hola*, Ernesto. Beautiful bougainvillea here."

"You are?"

"Felicia today."

He continued raking as she talked. Most likely the grounds were on camera, so she had to make this quick.

"I need to get word to Gisella—Agent Reyes—that the takedown is tonight."

Ernesto stopped digging and looked at her, his eyes boring into hers. "Tonight? You are all ready?"

"Yes, it will happen with the evening meal. All five points of contact will be heavily sedated for at least two hours. Enough time for the agency to move in."

Ernesto reached down and pulled out a weed by the roots. "Are there any girls in the basement right now?"

Tatiana tried not to look shocked. Girls in the basement? "I don't know," she answered.

"Well, no woman in that house is there willingly. I'll get the message out this morning. You better go now. Be safe." He resumed cultivating the flowerbed as Tatiana turned to leave.

A few minutes later, Tatiana found the kitchen empty. She stopped for a glass of water when she heard two men's voices just outside.

"He's a fed, boss. What do you want us to do?" said one of the guards.

"We'll need to find out what he knows and how he got here," said Andrej. "Go out and get him. Put him in a cell in the basement. I'll be down in a while."

When Andrej came storming into the kitchen seconds later, Tatiana yelped and dropped a handful of cookies on the floor.

"So sorry, I was just so hungry!" She motioned to pick them up, but Andrej barked, "Stop! You're lucky I don't throw you out right now. Do you know what I do with thieves in this house?"

"So sorry, *jefe*, so sorry!" Tatiana mewled, eyeing the floor and the jumbled mess of cookies.

"Stop saying you're sorry!" He grabbed Tatiana by the arm and yanked her up against his lean, hard body. Taking ahold of her ponytail, he held her face close to his. "I haven't seen you do any work since you got here. Are you going to give me a run for my money, you little vixen?" He cupped her bottom in his free hand, pulling her even tighter against him and laughed.

Then just as quickly, he pushed her away. "Get yourself cleaned up.

You're not working for Ramona anymore. I want you in my bedroom after my meeting."

Tatiana motioned to pick up the cookies, but he stopped her. "I said, go get yourself cleaned up. Leave that for Lisette. I want you in an evening gown. Ramona has plenty."

As Tatiana left the kitchen, she tried to get a good look outside for Ernesto. Most likely, the guard already had him, and there was no way she could warn him.

When the plane finally landed in Cabo, anxiety had Brett on edge. Maybe it was the fact that he wasn't used to this sort of thing, but he could have sworn he was picking up on Tatiana's fear. He'd thrown his vow to forget her out the window before he boarded the plane. All those therapy sessions had taught him one thing—face your fears, yes, but more importantly, face your emotions. The fact was that he loved Tatiana. For the first time in a long time, he could feel again, and his emotions were rushing in like a tsunami now.

Rodrigo's contact here, a woman named Lupe, had him picked up when he landed. He was instructed to look for a sign with his last name on it. The man smiled when Brett approached and held out his hand.

"*Señor* Johnson? *Yo soy* Filipo," he said as they shook.

"*Mucho gusto*, Filipo. I don't have any luggage, so we can go."

Brett followed Filipo to an old Cadillac. As they got in, he asked, "How far is the hacienda?"

"About thirty minutes."

When they pulled onto the highway a few minutes later, Brett happened to glance in the rearview mirror and saw a black SUV. His blood pressure shot up, then he chided himself. He was just overtired and possibly overly paranoid in this unfamiliar environment. He leaned back in the car seat and closed his eyes, thinking about Tatiana.

Tatiana returned to her room and sat down on her bed, trying to get her bearings. Ernesto had been found out, which could mean that she and Ramona were next. She had to warn Ramona somehow, and what the hell was she going to do with Andrej? She thought about Brett and his tender embrace, wishing he were here now.

A dramatic jolt startled Brett awake.

"*Ay, no!*" cried Filipo as the SUV rammed them a second time. He floored the Cadillac, but it was no match for the other vehicle, which quickly gained on them, coming upon their left side and pushing the Cadillac to the right and off the road. The older vehicle bumped over the shoulder and pitched into a field, coming to a halt. Filipo pressed on the gas, but the tires only spun.

Two men were at Brett's door in no time. With the butt of a gun, one of the men broke the glass and reached in to open the door. He grabbed Brett by the arm and pulled him out of the car, the gun pressed against his temple.

"Leave that one alive as a message," the gunman told the other man at Filipo's window. "The boss only wants the American."

There was no point in Brett playing dumb. "*Quien es el jefe?* Vargas?" he asked.

"You speak Spanish, gringo. And you know the *jefe*. Tell him what he wants to know, maybe you get off easy." He jerked Brett to the SUV and threw him in the back. "Any sudden movements, and I shoot your knee caps."

27

The SUV came to a stop at some sort of compound, with armed guards. The two men got out, leaving Brett in the car for what seemed like an hour—with the windows closed. It had to be about 90 outside, and it was more than 100 degrees in the car. He started to sweat profusely.

When the guard finally ordered him to get out, Brett was lightheaded. The guard led him toward a big trailer, which looked like headquarters for the compound. As he walked up the trailer's stairs, Brett wondered what Vargas wanted with him.

"*Señor* Johnson, welcome," said a muscular Mexican with a goatee and bald head as Brett stood before him. He was seated in an oversized armchair, a white Chihuahua in one arm. Brett couldn't help but stare at the creature, which growled at him. At least it wasn't a pitbull, but those pointy teeth looked painful.

The man laughed. "You never seen a dog before, *Señor* Johnson? Say *hola* to Lolita."

Brett eyed the dog.

"You deaf? Say *hola* to Lolita," commanded Vargas. "She doesn't like it when you hurt her feelings."

"*Hola*," Brett said to the dog, then asked Vargas, "So, what do you want?"

"Not so fast. Let's get to know each other first. Raul, where are *Señor* Johnson's belongings?"

The guard handed Vargas Tatiana's cellphone and Brett's wallet. He grinned when he flipped open the wallet to expose Brett's driver's license, taken just after he'd been surfing.

"What do they call you in California? A surfer dude? A surfer bum?"

"That would be beach bum."

"Oh, yes. The American expressions. So unimaginative."

Vargas opened Tatiana's phone next and started examining the numbers. "You check out this 310 number, Raul?"

"*Si*, boss, it was some low-level thug—didn't know anything more than we know."

"And this other number? Is that who I think it is?" He smirked. "When I get ahold of her, I am going to rip each of her appendages from her body, one by one."

Brett tried not to react, but he couldn't help jerking when Vargas said this.

"*Mierda*, surfer dude! Isn't she a little old for you?"

He was perhaps referring to Gisella, Brett thought. He tried to keep an impartial look on his face.

"Don't worry, we will find your friend who owns the phone, too." Vargas placed his dog on the floor. "Time to start talking now, *Señor* Johnson."

The door to Tatiana's tiny room flew open. It was Ramona, with Andrej glued to her side.

"We've come to pick out your attire." He grinned.

"So sorry, *Señora Ramona*." Tatiana immediately fell into her submissive character. "I did not mean to spill the cookies. You can take the cookies out of my pay."

"Enough about those damn cookies!" Andrej fumed and yanked Tatiana from the bed to her feet. He looked accusingly at Ramona. "I thought you said you vetted her?"

"I did. She came from the same agency you always use, and I had her searched."

Andrej spied Tatiana's toiletry bag and snapped it up. He yanked out her toothpaste and brushes and threw them on the bed, then pulled out the bag's lining. When he started shaking the bag upside down, Tatiana hoped that no powder had leaked out of the ketamine baggie.

"I told you! She's clean."

He looked Tatiana up and down. "We'll see about that. Forget her outfit."

"Andrej, baby, let's go have some fun, just you and me."

Andrej grabbed Ramona's hair and yanked her sideways. "Don't you dare talk back to me. You know what happens."

"I didn't mean to talk back, baby, I just want to be with you. That's all."

"Tell you what. I'm going to take care of this whore, then you and I can spend the rest of the day and night together. Jerome!" he bellowed to a guard at the foot of the stairs.

The guard came running up. "Yes, boss?"

Andrej flung Ramona at him. "Put her in her room and guard the door. I don't want to be disturbed."

Jerome led Ramona away, and Tatiana tried to still her panic and need to run.

"Now." He turned to her. "We're going to find out all about you." He squeezed hard on Tatiana's bottom, pushing her toward his room. Once inside, he deadbolted the door.

"Take off your clothing."

"No."

He rubbed his palms together. They stood there, eyeing one another. Andrej moved forward as Tatiana backed up, searching with her peripheral vision for some sort of weapon.

He laughed. "You're not going anywhere, except back to your room when we're done."

Andrej lunged at her and sent them both crashing onto the marble tile. Tatiana's back smashed painfully on the unforgiving floor. He reached down and tried to pull up her maid's skirt, but she wriggled and grabbed his sides, squeezing, which caused him to jerk up. She sent her right knee up into his private parts, and he howled. Wiggling out from underneath him, she stood and scanned the room, her eyes falling on a small metal statue. She ran to grab it and charged back at Andrej, hitting him on the side of the head. The shock in his eyes gave way to pain as his head fell back on the floor and he passed out. Tatiana felt for a pulse. Still alive.

Rearranging her skirt, she unbolted the door and left the room, easing the door behind her. The guard outside of Ramona's bedroom door looked up, surprised, when Tatiana approached.

"*El jefe* wants Ramona now," she said, looking down at the ground as she talked.

"I only take orders from the boss."

Tatiana nodded. "He is busy right now." She snuck a look at the guard and willed herself to redden. She waited for his hesitation, then added, "He ordered me to come tell you."

Another guard approached, and he said to him, "Antonio, this girl is saying the boss wants to see Ramona." Tatiana felt relief hearing Antonio's name—the guard on their side.

"We only take orders from the boss."

"That's what I told her."

Antonio went over to Andrej's door and rapped and waited. "I better check with him first."

A minute later, Antonio exited the room. "He says he wants both women right away. You're supposed to be on lunch now. I'll take care of this."

Looking relieved to be on break, Jerome nodded and left. Antonio opened Ramona's door and found her standing there.

Ramona peered into the hallway. "What's going on? Are you okay, Tatiana?"

"She's okay, but Andrej isn't," said Antonio.

"We need him alive," Ramona reminded them.

"He's alive," said Tatiana.

"The rest of the guards are eating lunch right now, so the plan is still on track," said Antonio.

"But I don't think Ernesto had a chance to get word to Gisella," Tatiana said. "Andrej found out he's with the agency. So, we're flying alone here."

"They're holding him in the basement," Antonio added. "With the delivery of girls that came last night."

"Well, at least we've got Andrej with his hands full," said Ramona. "We have to get word out. Andrej has a cell jammer going at all times, but he has a hidden landline in his bedroom."

"Let me lead," said Antonio, pushing the door open to Andrej's room.

Tatiana gasped. It was empty. "I don't understand. I hit him hard!"

Ramona went to Andrej's desk and pointed to a bottom drawer. "The phone is in there. Can you shoot the lock, Antonio?"

The guard pointed his gun at the desk as a shot rang out. He crumpled to the floor.

Andrej stood in the doorway with a gun in his hand, bleeding from the side of his head.

Ramona moved to where Antonio lay bleeding, but Andrej pointed the gun at her and warned, "You touch your boyfriend, I will blow his and your brains out. You don't think I know, you slut? I see the way you look at him."

"Darling, that's not true. I only have eyes for you."

"Don't darling me." Andrej weaved slightly in the doorway and aimed at Ramona as he began to pull the trigger.

Tatiana lunged toward Ramona, pushing her to the side. The bullet ricocheted off a table. Then Tatiana ran at Andrej, grabbing him by the middle and knocking him off balance to the floor. His head hit the marble, and he yelled, taking a swing at her face with the gun. She moved her head, but not in enough time to miss getting hit in the chin. The impact sent lightning bolts of pain throughout her head. When her eyes focused again, she stared into the butt of Andrej's gun. A half-second later, a shot rang out, and Andrej's head fell to the floor, a bullet hole in his forehead. His body went flat underneath Tatiana.

Ramona stood over them, Antonio's gun still trained on Andrej, a look of finality on her face.

Tatiana got up off him and felt for a pulse. "He's gone," she said, taking the pistol from her hands.

Antonio moaned then, and Ramona ran to his side. "We've got to get him help."

"Okay, watch out. I'm going to blow that bottom drawer open." Tatiana aimed at the desk and took a shot, sending wood splinters flying. She pulled out the phone, and dialed Gisella's number.

"It's Tatiana."

"My God, are you okay?"

Tatiana told Gisella what had occurred and gave her their location. "We need an ambulance."

"Storvosky? He is still alive?"

Tatiana didn't answer at first.

"Ramona had to shoot him. He was going to kill me. But we can hopefully piece together enough from the guards to pinpoint Vargas's location. We'll figure out where he is."

"I hope so. He has your surfer boyfriend."

28

"Tatiana, you there? Stay put. We're coming to get you. Then we'll go find Vargas. I want him just as much as you do."

Oh, no you don't, thought Tatiana. Determination coursed through her veins at the thought of Brett at Vargas's mercy.

"We'll be there in twenty minutes tops. You hear me?"

Tatiana hung up the phone.

Ramona looked up, her face streaked with mascara, her eyes deep pools of worry as she pressed a towel into Antonio's wound. "I don't think he can lose much more blood."

"You care for him, don't you?"

For a microsecond, Ramona looked about to protest, but instead she admitted, "He's been so good to me. I never thought after all these years undercover that I could fall in love, especially this quickly, but I did."

Tatiana put her hand on Ramona's shoulder. "The ambulance should be here any minute. Do you have any idea where Vargas is?"

"I don't know for sure, but there's a warehouse near here that he uses. Corner of Fidelio and La Manta."

Tatiana ran out of the room and downstairs, gun drawn. No guards in sight. She went back to the kitchen where she found Lisette, a roll of duct tape in her hands and the guards passed out on the floor, their hands and feet bound, and mouths covered.

Already distraught, Lisette gasped when she saw Tatiana's face. *"Dios mío! Qué pasó?"*

"Andrej is dead, but Antonio has been shot. Ramona has it under control until the ambulance gets here."

"You're leaving?"

"Tell Gisella that Ramona knows where I'm headed. I need a car."

"The boss has many cars. Antonio left the Maserati out. The keys are hanging by the back door."

Tatiana grabbed the keys and left. She'd never been in a Maserati, much less driven one. She stuck the key in the ignition. The car fired to life and she hit the gas, the back of her head smacking on the seat. She hit the brakes, then tapped lightly on the gas and carefully made her way down the mansion's circular drive.

Once out on the open road, she gave the Maserati more gas, marveling at how everything flew by in a blur. She had no idea what she'd do when she got to the warehouse, but she didn't care. She only knew that she had an overwhelming urge to make sure Brett was okay.

When Tatiana reached the building, she decided to drive right up front. Vargas would think it was Andrej or one of his people. She pulled up and revved the engine.

After a few seconds, a guard approached, leaning down on the driver's side. She opened the tinted window, and his eyes flew open at the gun in his face.

"Callate, or I will shoot your face off." Tatiana warned the guard. "I'm going to turn off the car and get out. If your boss asks who it is, say you're bringing in Storvosky. Don't, and I'll kill you. Give me your gun. Do it slowly."

Anger filled the guard's eyes as he removed his gun from a side holster and handed it to Tatiana.

She put it on the passenger side floor and turned off the car, then motioned for him to step back as she exited. Pointing to the door of the warehouse, she gestured for him to head that way.

When the guard pulled open the door, she heard Vargas ask in Spanish who had arrived. She stuck the gun in the guard's side, and he replied, *"Es el Jefe!"*

"Don't keep him waiting, come in."

Tatiana pushed the guard through the doorway, the gun in his back and entered the warehouse. Her heart lurched when she saw Brett tied to a chair, his head slumped forward. She resisted the urge to run to him.

Vargas stood up from the armchair he'd been sitting in. "I'm sorry boss, she had the Maserati."

"The Maserati, maybe she's Andrej's new girlfriend?" Vargas's eyes were steely. His dog sat at his feet.

Tatiana's mind raced as to what to do. "Let him go," she said evenly.

"Or you'll what, *chica*? Shoot my guard? I have plenty more where he comes from."

A gun rammed into Tatiana's back, and a strong hand grabbed the gun from her grasp.

"As I was saying, I have extra guards." Vargas motioned to the man holding her arm, who then turned and shot the guard who had let her in. "And I don't tolerate incompetence. But you know all these things ICE agent Romero."

Tatiana held her breath as the guard brought her closer to Vargas.

"Nasty bruise there, *chica*. Who did you piss off? When it comes to getting men angry, you learned from the best. Where is your *puta* boss, anyway?"

Tatiana remained silent, and irritation sparked in his eyes. Vargas reached for her chin and squeezed. She winced, but stood steady. How she wished that Brett would make a sound, so she knew he was alive.

"You're hurting my feelings, Agent Romero. I thought you came here to visit me, but I think you're more interested in the surfer bum. You were too late for him, by the way."

The thought of Brett dead filled Tatiana with searing rage. She struggled unsuccessfully to free herself from the guard's strong arms and let out an angry yell.

Vargas jumped back and laughed. "That's the spirit, *chica*! Let's get to it. I have other plans for today."

He looked around the warehouse. "Raul! Pedro! I need a little help here. Things are going to get bloody." There was no answer, and a flash of knowing passed across Vargas's face just as the shot rang out. The bullet hit him in the chest, sending him flying to the floor with a thud. The guard who had been holding Tatiana started to run, but a bullet hit him in the shoulder, and he cried out in pain.

In seconds, FBI agents swarmed the warehouse, and Gisella burst through the door. "*Mija*, I told you to wait!"

Tatiana ran to Brett's side, praying for signs of life. She checked. Thank God he had a pulse. His legs had what looked like bloody dog bites, but no signs of gunshot wounds. As she kneeled in front of him, tears clouding her vision, he stirred and opened his eyes. "What happened?" he said groggily. Relief propelled her forward as she rushed to untie him.

Once she freed him, Tatiana wrapped her arms around Brett. They remained that way for a long time, Tatiana's relief soon transforming to resolve.

29

"If you were working for me, I'd give you a big reprimand right now. But since you're not, I won't bother," said Gisella when Tatiana and Brett pulled apart. "Looks like we took down the entire operation. What's left of Storvosky's and Vargas's shared crew are in custody. We just found a big heroin stash here in the warehouse, and the girls being held at the mansion are being freed."

Tatiana stood there not saying anything, and Gisella raised an eyebrow. "You okay? Why don't you both go to the hospital. I'll get your statements later."

Tatiana nodded, and she and Brett left the warehouse. When she opened the door to the Maserati, Brett commented, "I see we're going to the hospital in style."

Tatiana got in without saying a word, and Brett's heart hitched. "You're quiet," he said as he settled in the seat. "Thanks for coming to my rescue."

"This was all my fault." Tatiana spoke in a low voice as she maneuvered the car out of the parking lot and headed for the hospital in Cabo. "It's always my fault."

"Look, we're alive. And Vargas and that Russian guy are dead. We should be celebrating."

Tatiana didn't reply.

When Tatiana was cleared with only a badly bruised chin, she left the hospital as fast as possible. Better to leave now before she weakened and went to see Brett. She texted Gisella and asked her to keep an eye on him.

Tatiana returned to the hacienda to get the cash she had Lupe hold for her. The older woman commented, "I hear you got your men, so to speak. And rescued several young women. Good work."

"Thank you," said Tatiana. "How is Antonio?"

"He is going to make it. Ramona won't leave his side. And your friend? How is he?"

Tatiana averted her eyes and said, "He's going to be okay. Do you have a driver to take me to the airport?"

"I can have Maria Elena drive you. You don't wish to stay the night and make sure your friend is okay before leaving?"

"I must get back to my job and my *abuelita*," said Tatiana.

"Oh, she isn't well? I'm sorry to hear that."

"No, yes, no. She will be concerned about me. I eat dinner with her several times a week."

"I see," said Lupe, eyeing Tatiana closely. "Very well, I will have Maria Elena take you to the airport right away. Perhaps you'll even be able to visit your *abuelita* before she goes to bed for the night."

As Lupe bustled away, Tatiana felt ashamed at herself for lying. There was no way she could go see her grandmother. *Abuelita* would know immediately that something was wrong. Tatiana wouldn't be able to stop herself from telling her everything, and then her grandmother would probably order her to return and face Brett.

"Tatiana, you come out here right now. You are going to the funeral. You must show respect for your mother." *Abuelita* rapped hard on Tatiana's bedroom door.

"What respect did she show me, *abuelita*? She whored around with her boyfriends and never cared if I was alive or dead. And now she overdoses a week before my graduation."

Abuelita was silent for a moment, and then said in a low tone, "You will go to the funeral with me, and you will hold your head high. Or you can pack your things and leave."

Tatiana opened the door. "Fine. But don't expect me to cry."

When Brett awoke hours after being admitted to the hospital, it was dark outside. A nurse stood over his bed, making notes in his chart.

"You're awake," she said in English. "That is good. You have a concussion. And the dog bites had to be stitched up."

"I came in with a woman. Long black hair. Her chin was hurt?"

"Yes, she left a few hours ago. They discharged her."

"Did she leave any messages?"

"No, I'm sorry. Rest now, *Señor* Johnson. It is important for your head to heal."

Brett found himself sinking into a fuzzy haze as he drifted off.

On the third day in the hospital, Brett felt more like himself. The doctors determined that he could go home. He was trying to figure out how to do that when Gisella charged into his room.

"Good to see you're okay," she said. "I've been checking on you. The FBI has arranged for transport back to the States. The doc says you can travel tomorrow, if that sounds good?"

"Fucking incredible."

"I wish we could compensate you more, but at least we can cover your hospital bills. I'm really sorry. Keep in touch and let me know if there are any other medical bills."

"Where the hell is Tatiana?"

Gisella shifted her footing and sighed. She studied Brett, her eyes sincere. "Tatiana has issues, you know that. About being abandoned. I think almost losing you has scared her away."

"What kind of fucked up logic is that?"

"There is no logic," said Gisella. "Just talk to her when you get home. She's back at her post on the beach."

"I'll think about it."

"Good." Gisella started to walk out of the room.

"Wait," Brett called out after her. "That social security number you had Tatiana memorize. That wasn't about the case, was it?"

"Tatiana said you were a natural for this work." Gisella smiled. "No, the social security number has nothing to do with the case."

"Have you talked to her about it yet?"

"You have my permission to do so," said Gisella.

"That's coercion, you know."

Gisella laughed. "I know."

30

Brett was back on his boat and groped in the dark for his clock. Five o'clock in the morning. In another hour, Tatiana would leave her post. He got up and dressed, then splashed water on his face and gingerly touched the lump on the back of his head. It seemed slightly smaller. He went to his safe and extracted Tatiana's gun, badge and wallet. He grabbed his keys and headed out.

Once in the van, Brett ran through his plan. He would make this brief. Give Tatiana her things and leave.

When he got to Imperial Beach, the moon shined bright. As he headed down toward the beach, he saw her silhouette. She stood looking out at the ocean. When he was just a few feet away, he half expected her to turn around, but she didn't move.

Since Tatiana had gotten back, she'd been walking around in a fog. She hadn't even gone to see her grandmother. Instead, she told her she had a cold and would come when she got better. When would that be? When would she ever feel better about Brett?

Tatiana felt someone right behind her and turned around. She couldn't mask the joy that lit up her insides at the sight of him.

"Brett," she started, "let me explain."

"What is there to explain?" He set her things in the sand and then put a hand to the back of his head. He was clearly in pain.

Tatiana reached out. "Why don't you sit down?"

Brett pulled back. "You left me in a Mexican hospital without a word. Now you want me to believe you care?"

"It's not an act! I do care. I just—"

All the frustration Brett had been feeling since this dance with Tatiana first began came rushing to the surface. "You just what, Tatiana? Explain it to me. You can't, can you? Because the truth is, you're so busy feeling sorry for poor Tatiana that you can't see what's right in front of you. Not me, not Gisella. We don't all have wonderful lives, Tatiana! We do our best to survive, and we take the precious gifts that come to us in the form of other people. But you are so closed off, nothing can break through that wall."

They stared at each other silently, then Brett turned to leave, stopping short when Tatiana cried out, "You tell me that I feel sorry for myself about my drug addict mother and no father. What about you? You had a sister who you loved, and thanks to your drug addict brother, she's gone. Killed right before your eyes. You live with survivor's guilt every day, and you pretend like nothing happened."

Brett stopped walking. He turned, astounded at her words.

"I love you, *hombre,* and I'm not going to let you go like this." Tatiana held her breath. She wished now she hadn't mentioned his sister. It was probably the most sensitive button of his she could have pushed. Why did she always mess things up? "Will you tell me about your family?" Tatiana almost whispered.

Brett looked directly at Tatiana. Finally, he asked, "Did you say you love me?"

"Yes, and I don't know what I'm supposed to do. Or not supposed to do. All I know is that I don't want to live without you."

Brett strode to her. "I love you, too," he said, cradling her face in his hands as tears glistened in her eyes.

They sat down in the wet sand as the tide receded and the sun painted its way up the horizon. Tatiana slid close to Brett, until she was pressed against him.

"Take your time. I've got all day."

Brett took a deep breath and began.

"I grew up in La Jolla with a brother named Nick and a sister, Carolina. We were your typical upper middle-class family—until Nick got involved in drugs. He started out slow but eventually graduated to meth. His drug abuse and the resulting lies and stealing took a toll on my parents. He stole family heirlooms and sold them for drug money, as well as electronics or whatever he could get his hands on. At one point, my dad talked him into going in for rehab and paid for it. But Nick was soon back on the street hustling for drugs. Although I don't think Nick's drug problem caused my dad's heart attack, it didn't help. It was massive. My mom called 911, but he died before they arrived."

Brett stopped and took a handful of sand, letting the grains filter through his fingers before resuming. "Losing my dad made my mom more determined than ever to save Nick. She talked him into another round of rehab and started giving him money in hopes that he'd get it together. Finally, Mom realized trying to help was hopeless, and she told Nick to leave and not come back until he got his life together."

Brett took a deep breath and continued. "As the youngest, cutting ties with Nick was hard on Carolina. She was always the peacekeeper in the family, and she saw a lot of the struggle between mom and Nick, because she was living at home. One night, I was visiting while mom was out with some friends. It was just me and Carolina in the house. I was in the garage gathering some tools so I could make a few home repairs for my mom. During that time, Nick came to the door with two of his friends, and Carolina let them in."

Tatiana's heart clutched when Brett stopped and stifled a sob. She took his hands in hers and murmured, "It's okay if you don't want to continue."

"No, it's time," he said. "The guys my brother was with were all hopped up on meth. They had come to try and get some money out of my mom, and one of them had a gun. When they found out she wasn't there, they started getting rough with Carolina. I was coming back from the garage when I heard her scream." Brett paused.

"I don't need all the details," Tatiana said.

"I tried to stop them from hurting her. One had torn the buttons from her blouse. When Nick realized what was about to happen, he tried to stop them, too, but everything got crazy. Somehow in the struggle, Carolina and Nick got shot. When my mom discovered them, she was never the same after that. I know she tried to be there for me, but she just couldn't. I ended up putting her in a psychiatric facility. She contracted pneumonia a year ago, and it led to complications. She passed away. I think she no longer had the will to fight."

Brett stopped to look out at the ocean, grief covering his face.

"You got shot, too, didn't you?"

"Yeah, I did. I lost a lot of blood, but I survived. The only one."

"So that's why your boat is named Carolina."

"I bought the boat after what happened to Carolina. I wanted to honor her memory in some way, so I named the boat after her. I also wanted to make sure that I never forgot her." Brett rubbed the back of his head. "After that night, I just couldn't be in the house. What happened kept replaying, so I started living on the boat. I think I'm just going to sell the place."

Tatiana lifted Brett's hands to her lips and kissed them, then rested her head on his shoulder. They sat that way in silence for a time, until early morning surfers started to arrive. Then they decided to go back to Tatiana's house.

When Tatiana parked her bike out front of her house and waited for Brett to get out of his car, she thought how much strength he had. To have experienced such horror and still be standing.

Once inside the living room, Brett spoke first. "I've never talked with anyone about that night. Until now."

Tatiana moved closer, then kissed his mouth, softly, tentatively, the tenderness nearly overwhelming her. She wanted to caress his every wound, erase every wrong he'd ever felt. The desire to soothe his soul took hold of her heart, and all she wanted was to put a smile back on his face, hear one of his silly jokes.

Brett pulled her closer, gazing at her for several long minutes, then kissed her with such urgency, it felt as if her body was on fire.

"What do you want, Tatiana?" His voice was gruff. "Tell me."

Tatiana didn't know how to tell him what was in her heart and instead led him up the stairs to her bedroom. The morning light was peeking under the blinds, washing the room in a strange ethereal light. Brett sat on the edge of the bed, and Tatiana kneeled in front of him, removing the sandal from one of his feet, then unbuckling and removing the other one. She caressed his muscled legs, marveling at their strength and picturing him balanced on a surfboard riding a wave, the sunlight glistening on his tan, wet skin.

He lay back on the bed and Tatiana pushed his T-shirt up his body and helped it off. Her lips traveled across his chest, the skin so warm, then found his neck. He closed his eyes, not speaking, and she was grateful for that. It was as if they both didn't want to break the spell.

Tatiana began unzipping the front of his pants, then hesitated. Brett lifted his head slightly and looked at her, then started to get up. She pushed him back on the bed, and he smiled, closing his eyes once again and reaching down to stroke her hair. Tatiana guided his pants off, then his briefs, revealing his erection. At the sight, her heart hammered against her ribs. She took him between her hands, moving in slow motion as he moaned. Then she stood and removed her clothes, until she stood naked before him in the early morning light.

Brett raised up on one hand to look at her. "You're so beautiful," he said.

When she climbed onto this man she loved, moving her body in gentle rhythm while his strong hands gripped her bottom, she felt him grow larger and harder inside of her as he thrust himself deep. It seemed to only take a moment before they exchanged both their passion and hearts, waves of desire wiping out everything but one another.

When they awoke, still entangled in one other, it was the middle of the afternoon.

"I think my arm is asleep," said Brett.

Tatiana sat up, her hair sweeping across his chest as she did so. "It'll probably help if I stop lying on it," she said. "Are you hungry? I think I have some frozen pizza."

"Sounds like a feast." Brett smiled up at her, and Tatiana's heart eased at the sight.

"Feeling better?"

"I'm feeling great. Although I could use a couple of aspirin for this headache."

"Stay right there," she said, popping up and leaving the room.

When she returned, Brett had an odd look on his face. "There's something I just remembered that I need to tell you. Actually, it's something Gisella wants me to tell you."

"Is she okay?" Tatiana sat down on the bed and handed him the water and aspirin.

"It's actually good news," Brett said, taking the aspirin.

"Oh?"

"Remember that number you memorized from her safe?"

"The social security number?"

"Yes. It belongs to someone important to you. The man in the photo."

Tatiana didn't understand at first, then suddenly she realized what he was saying. "Oh, my God! That's my father? Gisella found him?"

"She didn't give me the details, but yes, she did. She probably wanted you to memorize his social in case something happened to her."

Tatiana's mind reeled at the news. "What do I do?"

"What do you want to do?"

"I don't know. I...It would be good to know who he is after all these years. I've always wondered."

"Then look him up."

Tatiana got out of bed and went to her desk, opening her laptop. She put in her ICE security credentials and typed in the social security number, holding her breath while the system generated the information. She expected to see a mugshot pop up, but what appeared on the screen shocked her.

Brett came up behind her. "You sure you put in the right number?"

Tatiana checked the number again. "I'm positive."

Brett read off the screen. "Judge Robert Rodriguez. You going to introduce yourself?"

"Maybe someday." Tatiana pushed her chair back from the desk.

Brett looked at her surprised.

"I already have my family," she said. "This man doesn't know me, and probably has no idea I even exist. I'm not sure I want to disrupt his life. Knowing this puts things into perspective—including my choice in careers. But, really, *abuelita* raised me, and Gisella has been like a mother to me. And then there's you. You're my family, Brett. I've got what I've always wanted. And right now, there's something I really want to do."

"What?"

"Can you teach me to surf?"

Brett grinned. "Of course."

EPILOGUE

Brett and Tatiana's stories are complete, but Rodrigo's is just beginning...

Rodrigo was sure he had come to the right street. The guy had been clear. He'd been in Orange County enough times to know where McFadden was. The guy told him to wait in front of a warehouse. Probably busy earlier in the evening, the place was empty now at three in the morning. Getting bored, Rodrigo reached for a cigarette and lit it, inhaling deeply. Monica hated that he smoked. Actually, she hated just about everything he did, except for bringing in the *dinero*.

The black sedan that pulled up gave Rodrigo a chill. It wasn't good when that happened. He realized now that he should have brought one of his guns. This customer had been a referral, but maybe packing a piece would have been a good idea.

He sucked in his breath when he saw who got out of the car. A real looker. Long legs and blond hair. She walked up to his Chevy, her hair catching rays of light from the streetlamps.

"Mr. Rodrigo," she said, with an accent. What was that, Russian? "You have the card?"

"I sure do, *hermosa*," Rodrigo said, handing her a brown paper bag containing the social security card the guy had ordered earlier that day.

She examined it with the light from her cellphone. "It looks good. I trust you can't be tied back to this card? I was told you use strict discretion."

"Always, *hermosa*." He looked her up and down, wondering if she preferred *cerveza*, or vodka. Isn't that what the Russians drank?

"Good, because if it is tied back to you in any way, you'll be dead before you can cheat on your girlfriend again. And if you call me *hermosa* one more time, I will squeeze your little balls off."

Rodrigo stared after her as she got into the car and sped away. He sat there, speechless, until he jumped at a sharp pain on his leg. The cigarette's ember had burned a hole in his pants.

See what happens with Rodrigo in *Discovered Liaisons*.

A NOTE FOR YOU

Dear Reading Gem,

Thanks for spending time with me, Tatiana and Brett! While each of the books in **the Discovered Truth Series** can be read as a standalone, it's fun to experience the progression and get to know the characters. The series progresses as minor characters introduced in each book become main characters in subsequent books. It's exciting to see what they'll do next!

The Discovered Truth series features complex, gutsy women and equally complicated, charismatic men who find themselves immersed in dangerous and intriguing modern-day challenges, such as human trafficking, drug smuggling, national security threats, and identity theft. When the heroine and hero meet, worlds collide and sparks fly, kindling unforgettable romance and intrigue.

If you like the series, please leave a review on any book review platform. Your opinion matters and is incredibly powerful.

Thanks again and talk soon!

STAY ENLIGHTENED

Thanks for reading! Let's stay in touch. In appreciation of you, I post updates, insider information, and sneak peeks of upcoming books on my website at https://www.juliebawdendavis.com/fiction. You can also email me at Julie@JulieBawdenDavis.com, follow me on Facebook, and find me on Amazon.

Even better, you can join my VIP Reading Gems mailing list here. I also created a Facebook group especially for you! Join Julie's Reading Gems to get the inside scoop on what's going on with the Discovered Truth Series. Find out how characters are created, and what they might do next. I also ask for Reading Gem opinions on upcoming covers and even plot twists. And there are contests and giveaways!

Escape to Unforgettable Romance and Intrigue...

BOOKS IN THE DISCOVERED TRUTH SERIES

Box Sets

The Discovered Truth Series Box Set Books 1-4
The Discovered Truth Series Box Set Books 5-8
The Discovered Truth Series Box Set Books 9-12
The Discovered Truth Series Box Set Books 13-16

www.ingramcontent.com/pod-product-compliance
Lightning Source LLC
Chambersburg PA
CBHW022125170626
46808CB00002B/844